# Period Pieces

selected by
**ERZSI DEÀK**
and
**KRISTIN EMBRY LITCHMAN**

HarperCollins*Publishers*

Library of Congress Cataloging-in-Publication Data
Period pieces : stories for girls / selected by Erzsi Deàk and
Kristin Embry Litchman.
    p.   cm.
    Summary: A collection of twelve stories about girls' expe-
riences as they begin to menstruate.
    ISBN 0-06-623796-3 — ISBN 0-06-623797-1 (lib. bdg.)
    1. Menstruation—Juvenile fiction. 2. Children's stories,
American. [1. Menstruation—Fiction. 2. Short stories.]
I. Deàk, Erzsi.  II. Litchman, Kristin Embry.
PZ5 .P415 2003               2002017295
[Fic]—dc21                   CIP
                          AC

Typography by Amy Ryan
1  2  3  4  5  6  7  8  9  10

First Edition

For my fantastic granddaughters,
Hilary, Katja, Elizabeth,
and Rebekah, with love
—K. E. L.


For my family:
Charles, and especially my three girls,
Elisabeth, Nelly, and Esmée,
who patiently waited for me to quit typing
—E. D.

# Contents

# Introduction

Have you fallen off the wall? Seen George lately? Had the painters in? Does Auntie pay you a visit? Do Little Bears make you growl?

No matter what you call it, or what you say about it, getting your period is a big deal. What's it like to have one? Is it scary? Embarrassing? A pain in the neck? Exciting? A huge yawn? Can you hardly wait to "become a woman," or do you hope the day will never come?

Years ago, many girls weren't told that their bodies would change and start bleeding! Those first periods were often terrifying experiences.

Most girls today have a better time of it. Big sisters, friends, parents, teachers, nurses—everybody's got something to say about periods, whether it's superstition or folklore or hearsay or scientific facts with pictures and diagrams all about what happens inside girls' bodies as they grow into women.

But it's hard to diagram feelings. One day we got to talking with some other authors about how we felt when we first got our periods. Everybody wanted to tell a funny or scary or touching story. And we thought, Hey! Stories like these would make a great book!

So here they are—stories that share the life-changing experience common to all of us girls.

Erzsi Deák
Kristin Embry Litchman

# Period Pieces

# Period.

## April Halprin Wayland

It sounds so final.
Like things stop.
When you get it.

I know that when I finally get mine,
I'm going to be so thrilled I'm going to call it my
Exclamation Point.

# I Don't Wanna Hear It

### Kristin Embry Litchman

**LOS ALAMOS, NEW MEXICO, 1951**

We crouch in our secret hiding place, the crawl space beneath a government-owned stucco house. We enter by squeezing through a trapdoor in Madeline's hall closet. Light filters through the floorboards overhead. Angie's dim flashlight shows shadowy wood beams, boards, mysterious pipes, and spiderwebs.

Lots of spiderwebs.

I think of the black widow spider Billy brought to school in a bottle last week. "One bite and you die," he said with satisfaction, pointing out the scarlet hourglass on the stomach of the shiny black spider. Now, at our second club meeting, I huddle in the sandy dirt, keeping my head well clear of beams and

2

pipes. "Are there any black widows down here?"

"Nah," says Angie. "Just daddy longlegs."

I hope so. Angie should know; she and Madeline are twelve, a year older than me. Sometimes, though, they make up stuff to see if I believe it. If I do, they laugh at me.

Angie switches off her flashlight. "Let's save the batteries," she says. "Now nobody knows where we are."

Last week we planned the club, deciding on passwords and meeting times and other secret stuff.

"Let's tell secrets," Madeline says now. "I've got a good one. My cousin told me last summer. Did you know that when you grow up you bleed from your bottom?"

"Bleed?" I stare at her, appalled.

Angie has already heard this story. "Yup."

"Why?" I ask.

Angie shrugs. "Something to do with babies. All the big girls do it."

"All the time?" I ask. I can't believe such a thing could happen.

"No," says Angie. "Just for a few days."

"Every month for a few days," Madeline adds.

"When you go to the bathroom?"

"No, all the time for the few days."

*Spiders swing down from their webs.*

"You have to wear a thing like a diaper," says Madeline, "so the blood doesn't get all over."

*Spiders creep closer.*

"We can't wear diapers. We're too big."

"You'll have to when you get older. All girls bleed. You can't stop it." Madeline certainly sounds positive.

"Don't the boys have to bleed?"

"No."

"That's not fair!"

"That's the way it is."

"I don't believe it," I say, meaning that I won't believe it.

"It's true," insists Angie. She almost sounds convincing.

*Tickly legs crawl up my back.*

"I have to go now," I say. "I promised my mother I'd be back in half an hour." I didn't promise anything, but I have to get out of here.

"It's not half an hour yet," Angie protests.

I don't care. I also don't care if they kick me out of the club. I'm not all that crazy about secrets anymore.

I crawl recklessly into the dark, scraping my bare knees on unseen rocks and splintery boards, searching

4

for the way out. Finally, the others come, too, flashing the light.

I won't hear any more. I run all the way home, chasing that story out of my mind . . . and those spiders.

Weeks have passed. Angie and Madeline and I don't have the secret club anymore. We collect horse statues instead. Nobody mentions The Story again. Obviously they made it up.

Then, out of the blue one day, I hear it again.

"Kris?" says Mom, interrupting *Jill Has Two Ponies*, a book I'm reading for the third time. "Come help me make my bed. We need to have a little talk."

A little talk? She's never asked me to have a little talk before. As she flips a clean sheet over the bed and I grab its corners to tuck in, I feel like I'm back in the crawl space, with spiders creeping up my spine. I don't want to hear whatever she has to say. But I'm trapped. Her first words surprise me: "You know where the baby hamsters come from."

Of course I know about the baby hamsters that live in a wire-topped metal bread box in the bedroom I share with my sisters. I also know about the size of our black cat before the kittens were born in the carport cupboard. I even know about my youngest brother, remembering how fat Mom was before he arrived. What I don't know is how all the babies got inside the mothers.

Mom relates a tangled story involving the daddy and mommy hamsters and how the mommy hamster is ready to make babies at a certain time. She skips lightly over daddy and mommy humans, and somehow ends up with a tale of blood similar to the story Madeline and Angie had tried to feed me, but with bigger words.

"Becoming a woman is a miraculous thing," Mom says, beating up the pillows in a way that makes me doubt her enthusiasm for this part of her story. "Now, do you understand how menstruation works? Here, pull up your side of the bedspread."

"Um," I say, yanking out the wrinkles. I wonder: Do girl animals have menstruation, too? I don't remember seeing any diapers on hamsters and cats. I try to think how to ask about the resemblance between hamsters and humans, but Mom is too quick for me.

"Time to hang up the laundry," she says, whooshing out a big breath and heading for the bedroom door. "So, when something like that happens to you, let me know."

Mom's a writer; she makes up stories all the time.

Maybe she's making up this one. I hope so.

I race outside, across the meadow, and down to the schoolyard. I spend the afternoon pumping up a swing as hard as I can and concentrating on the horse I plan to buy someday when I'm rich, until The Story moves far back in my mind, where I don't have to think about it.

A month later, on an otherwise beautiful fall day, the school nurse appears in the doorway of our sixth-grade classroom, armed with a slide projector and a stack of pamphlets.

The boys are sent out of the way to the art room next door, where they are probably plastering their ears against the wall and soaking up every embarrassing word the nurse speaks. We girls scuffle our leather-soled shoes on the floor and stare at our desks.

The nurse hands a pamphlet to each of us. "Growing Up and Liking It" says the cover. The sketch of a box beneath the title mysteriously adds, "Modess . . . Because."

My younger sisters and I have often puzzled over those words, featured in ads in all the women's magazines. How can you know what Modess is Because for, if you don't know the Why in the first place?

I'm afraid the nurse is going to tell us Why now, but I shut my ears. I don't want The Story to be true.

The pamphlet features cheery photos of beautiful teenage girls, who are eating healthy foods, going for healthy walks, drinking glasses of healthy water. Bowel movements are also mentioned as being healthy, though without a photo.

The nurse closes the venetian blinds and turns on the slide projector. A diagram flashes onto the wall. It shows, says the nurse, what each of us looks like inside and what is going to happen to all of us, sooner or later. She marches through her story, stabbing each part of the diagram with our teacher's wooden pointer.

Eggs. Tubes. Uterus. Lining.

The same diagrams are in our pamphlets. The nurse has us track imaginary little eggs down the tubes, into the uterus and out again, accompanied by blood.

Blood. Every month.

I'm stunned by those diagrams. I can't escape. It's all there on the wall, and in a book, just like Angie and Madeline and my mother said.

The nurse tells us how we will deal with all this blood. We'll wear little elastic belts under our underpants, with hooks front and back. We'll fasten the long tails of thick, soft, paper pads called sanitary napkins through the hooks. ("Modess" turns out to be a brand of these napkins.)

She points out a pamphlet picture in which a beautiful teenage girl is cheerfully buying a "Modess . . . Because" box from a smiling teenage boy in a drugstore. I scrooch down, red-faced, behind my desk. Never will I buy these things, especially not at the drugstore, where somebody might know me.

As we head home from school, trailed by a fringe of lunatic boys, the other girls giggle and push one another. I run away from them all. I'm furious at the boys, who will never have to bleed like this; furious at my friends, who do not seem to mind their own fate.

I run all the way home and into my room. I lock my door and curl up on my bed.

Three times I've heard this story. Maybe it's true.

Or, I think, maybe it will never happen to me.

Yeah, that's it. I'm different from other girls.

Besides, none of the girls in my horse stories ever mentions this bleeding business.

I'm not going to think about it anymore.

Unless something happens to prove me wrong.

# White Pants

## Linda Sue Park

I do not have documented evidence that I was the last girl in seventh grade at O. W. Smith Upper Grade Center to get her period, but *somebody* had to be last, right? I'd have been a good bet. To begin with, I had skipped a grade, so I was a year younger than everyone else. I was small and skinny, and there is no metaphor for flatness flat enough to describe my chest.

All the other girls had breasts *and* periods. The code word for period was *George.* As in, "No, I can't sleep over tonight. *George* is visiting." Or, "I'm in such a crappy mood—*George* is bugging me." For a while I wondered if it was a code word just for the girls, or if the boys knew it, too. Then I heard Jim

Williams, one of the eighth graders, say, "It sure was crowded at the mall last night—me, Debbie, and *George*." Loud guffaws from the other guys. So much for a girls-only secret.

It seemed like every girl but me got excused from gym class once in a while, and every girl but me had a little plastic zippered pouch in her locker, very discreet except that everyone knew what it held. George stuff. I wasn't sure I wanted to get my period—my friends weren't at their best when they had theirs—but I did want one of those pouches. I wanted to be able to sigh heavily and say, "It's such a *drag* having *George* around." I considered faking it, but I was sure everyone would know I was lying. Like a sign would flash on my (flat) chest in neon letters: NO FRIEND OF MINE—SIGNED, GEORGE. Through fall and winter, I was plagued by both dread and impatience, not a pretty combination.

In spring a wing of the school was closed for construction. Some classes had to be moved to an elementary school two blocks away. I went there for the last class of the day, French with Mrs. Lunsberger. *M'dam* Lunsberger, as she insisted we call her.

I always walked there with Janice O'Neill. Our lockers were on the same hall, and we had English class together just before French. We'd go to our lockers, dump our English books, get our French stuff and our jackets, and head out the door.

But we never hurried. It was an unspoken agreement among all the kids. Everyone took at least ten minutes to walk the short distance, and we could have done it in five, easy. We'd also convinced *M'dam* that we had to leave class ten minutes early to make it back in time for the buses. A forty-five-minute class reduced to twenty-five minutes, twenty by the time we all got settled down.

One day in April the weather and the calendar weren't speaking to each other: It didn't feel like spring, the month before May, but more February-ish, raw and gray. In French class, we had twenty minutes of nouns. I liked this class a lot, liked the idea of learning another language, but sometimes I wondered if the French actually wanted anyone else to learn it. Like today—*M'dam* said *sea* and *river* are feminine, but *ocean* and *water* are masculine; I mean really, could it be any more confusing?

Then we headed back toward the main building to hit our lockers one last time before getting on the bus. There were a lot of kids walking, five or six classes, at least.

Janice and I were talking about our English teacher,

Mrs. Gregory. She wore pointy glasses and frowned a lot, so at the beginning of the year we'd been scared of her. But by now we'd figured out the frown was just an act and we really liked her. English was always my favorite class, anyway.

Behind us, Robby Vanderpost and Pete Blumberg were talking and laughing. They were getting louder and louder, but at first we ignored them.

Then Robby yelled, "There he is, I see him!"

"I see him, too," Pete yelled back.

I glanced at them over my shoulder. They were laughing so hard they were hanging on to each other, tripping and staggering around. Very funny. I shrugged and turned back to Janice.

"YEP, THERE HE IS!" Robby was practically roaring now.

"GOOD OL' *GEORGE*!" Pete yelled at the top of his lungs.

George? Janice and I looked at each other. Right away she dropped back half a step and took a quick peek at the critical area. "Your jacket," she muttered. "Take it off and tie it around your waist."

It was all happening too fast for me. My brain was at least ten thoughts behind: If it's George, it has to be Janice. It couldn't be me. But how did Janice know right away to look at me? Oh, *duh*. Because she knew it wasn't her. Oh, jeez. That means it's me. Oh, jeez.

And I'm wearing white pants.

Brand-new white low-rise flares with navy stitching. That morning when I'd put them on, I'd slouched fashionably in front of the full-length mirror for a few moments. No doubt about it, these pants were *hot*.

Not anymore. Now they were stained, and it would have been a tough call which was redder—the stain or my face.

I tied the arms of my jacket around my waist. My lips were pressed together tightly, to keep the panic and embarrassment that had erupted inside me from spewing out and making even more of a mess.

"That's good," Janice said. "You can't see . . . anything, now."

Great. So only Robby and Pete and probably a few dozen others had seen by then.

Somehow I made it home without crying. I ran upstairs to the bathroom, and that's where my mom found me, washing out the white pants in the tub with soap, water, and a few tears for good measure.

She took one look and said, "Oh, Linda Sue— what happened?"

Like I was going to relive the agony by telling her about it? I don't think so. Instead I screamed, "What do you THINK happened?" Then, in a moment of stunning originality, I stomped into my room and slammed the door.

By evening my tears were dried and my mom had hugged me and gone out and bought me a little plastic zippered pouch full of George stuff and everything was okay, except that, naturally, I could never return to O. W. Smith Upper Grade Center as long as I lived. My mom didn't seem to understand this. She was completely deaf to my pleas for a transfer to another school.

So there I was the next morning, miserable in blue denim jeans (I'd considered wearing black pants but decided that would be too obvious) and a longish sweatshirt, waiting for the teasing to begin. I was used to being teased—for having thick glasses, for being Asian, for the aforementioned upper-body topography—but this would be different. I couldn't help any of those things; that was just the way I was, and I'd always thought the teasing was stupid because it wasn't like I could *change* any of it.

But this time it wasn't something I *was*. It was something I'd *done*—or hadn't done. It didn't matter that I couldn't have predicted the timing. It was still my fault, and doubtless by now the entire school was ready to let me know what a complete idiot I was.

The morning passed one minute at a time, so slowly I was sure the wall clocks were broken. Were people looking at me? Were they snickering behind their hands, passing notes, nodding at one other knowingly? And what would happen after French, when Robby and Pete would be there?

Nobody said anything all morning. I accidentally let my guard down a little, talking and even laughing during lunch. But then I remembered the disgrace that awaited me, the public humiliation that could happen at any moment.

I walked to French with Janice. She didn't say anything. Well, she said a lot of things—about Mrs. Gregory's homework, and wasn't Bill Fulton cute, and was I going to the basketball game next Tuesday? Nothing about George. French class came and went, and as we walked back, I caught a glimpse of Robby and Pete tossing a football with some other guys.

Nothing happened. It wasn't just that no one mentioned it. Sometimes when people aren't talking about something, you know they're all *thinking* about it, and their not talking just makes things worse. This wasn't like that. People weren't talking about it, and they weren't thinking about it, either.

I almost felt cheated. A waste of a perfectly good fight with my mom, and a whole lot of worry for nothing.

Well, maybe not nothing. Thirty years later, two things remain. First, I'll never forget how George introduced himself to me.

And that was the last pair of white pants I ever owned.

# The Gentleman Cowboy
### Cynthia Leitich Smith

I rode at the top of the world, surrounded by the snow-dusted Colorado Rockies and valleys of wildflower-speckled grass. Ryan, my cowboy guide, rode a tawny beige horse in front of me. Popeye, my horse, walked a dirt trail between a rising mountain and a hundred-plus-foot drop-off. A steep drop-off, paid for. Yep, that's right, I thought, clutching the reins in one hand and the saddle horn in the other. My daddy put down his credit card so I could get this towering view. This beautiful, inspiring, towering view from the many steep, rocky, jagged, death-defying cliffs.

Okay, so I don't like heights. I'm from Kansas. Kansans are flatlanders. A couple of days earlier, my parents had driven me to Estes Park for our family vacation.

Because they thought I'd think this was fun.

"Um, Ryan?" I began. "Are you sure we're supposed to be up here?"

He flashed a warm grin over his shoulder. "Trust Popeye," Ryan said. "He's been on this trail tons of times."

Trust Popeye, I thought. It wasn't like I had much choice. He was a gorgeous horse, black with white spots, one over his right eye. What if he slipped, I wondered, on loose dirt and rocks, tumbling off the side of the mountain, taking me along for the ride? Maybe I'd fall off and crack my head open. Maybe I'd stay stuck in the saddle and Popeye would land on top of me, creating a tourist pancake. Studying the distant landscape of pines below, I tried to decide which would be worse.

"And stop looking down," Ryan added.

I gripped the reins tighter and leaned back in the leather saddle, sweating slightly in the July sunshine. My head ached, and my back muscles felt sore. Saddle sore, I figured. My thighs seemed heavy, and my stomach had begun to cramp. The fact that I had to pee only made things worse. But I stopped looking down.

Letting out a breath, I petted Popeye's coarse mane and looked at Ryan and his horse instead. Ryan was six feet tall and skinny, not much older than sixteen, which made him only three years older than me. He wore a sweat-stained western shirt, sun-bleached cowboy hat, and worn boots that seemed to grow out of the legs of his faded Levi's.

Unlike the boys back home, Ryan cared about more than just football. He told me all about his uncle who owned the stables. He told me all about his sisters—Rachel, Rebecca, Ronnie, and Reba—back home at their ranch in Wyoming. He said they bossed him around. I could tell he missed them.

"Almost there," he announced. "Just one more turn."

Trust Popeye, I thought again. I trusted Ryan, too, partly because he seemed to know what he was doing and partly because I'd never seen a boy that cute.

When we turned, the path opened to a valley split by a rushing stream. Ryan took off running on his horse, motioning for Popeye and me to gallop behind them. I kicked my boot heels into Popeye's sides, and off we went. My hind end bounced on the saddle, and I felt my hat fly off, still held to my neck by its tie. The horses carried us to the water and lowered their heads for a cool drink.

As the horses drank, it started to rain, an afternoon shower that would only make the rock slicker for Popeye. My stomach felt awful, and a pimple was about to erupt on the tip of my nose. I checked my watch. We were two hours out on a four-hour tour.

Ryan reached over and set my cowboy hat on my head. "Sorry about that last pass," he said. "I didn't mean to scare you. Most people who sign up to go horseback riding in the mountains . . . like the mountains. But I can take you a different way back. There's just one narrow patch, and it's only about ten minutes on the trail."

I tried not to let on how relieved I was. "Ten minutes?" I asked. "I can handle that." And I could, I told myself, just so long as I trusted Popeye and Ryan and made sure not to look down. My bigger problem was more personal. Between the bouncing, the trickling stream, and the rain, I couldn't wait another two hours for a real bathroom, or at least what passed for one at the stable.

"Are you ready to go again?" Ryan asked when the horses had drunk their fill.

"I have to pee first," I said. It was a firm announcement. The kind made by people not turning cranberry red, not wishing they were anywhere else on the planet.

"Oh!" Ryan exclaimed, like peeing was a new concept. "Why . . . why don't you go over there?" He pointed at a cluster of bushes and reached for my reins. "I'll just take the horses on a little walk."

I climbed down from Popeye and, as Ryan briskly guided the horses away, made my way to a leafy shrub. Wonderful, I thought. I will survive peeing outdoors. I will ride for the next two hours with my hand subtly covering my emerging nose zit. I will manage not to die of embarrassment.

Letting out a breath, I wiggled my jeans down and discovered what looked like *the* crisis of the day. I was bleeding, grossly and steadily, on my cotton undies. *Bleeding.*

I squinted at the mess, suddenly remembering The Talk from Mama and *It's Your Body!* from girls' gym. I couldn't believe it! I was cursed—blessed— for the very first time, so much so that I'd already bled through the back end of my stone-washed blue jeans two hours from the stables in the company of a sixteen-year-old boy. A cute, sweet, sixteen-year-old boy, whom I'd just met, who didn't tease like the boys back home, and who I'd been imagining was guiding me because he *liked* me, not because it was his summer job.

As the rain tapered off to a mist, a drop of blood

streaked down my inner thigh. I put myself together as best I could and strolled, mostly sideways, to meet Ryan and the horses. Then I climbed back onto Popeye's saddle and off we rode. How much blood was going to come out of me, anyway? I wondered. Could Ryan *smell* it?

"Wanna run?" he asked after a few moments.

"Nope," I said, ducking under a branch. "I'm not feeling so good."

Ryan slowed to ride alongside me. "You're sick?" he asked, brow drawn. "Just now, or since we left the stable?"

I flexed my fingers around my reins. It didn't seem fair to worry Ryan, and I'd been raised not to lie. But this . . . I couldn't. . . . "I . . . I'm not sick exactly," I stammered.

"Do you want to rest?" he replied. "You look sweaty."

I did not feel pretty. I did not want to rest, either. I wanted to return to my motel room as soon as possible without anybody but Mama knowing what had happened. "I'm not sick exactly," I said, "but could we take a quicker path?"

Ryan handed me a canteen. "Dizzy? Nauseous?"

I made a great show of watching myself unscrew the cap. "I'm a girl, and I'm not feeling so good." I took a sip of icy water. "It's a *girl* kind of thing."

"Oh," Ryan replied, not sounding too sure. And then, blushing, "Oh! Oh, right. That's totally okay. I mean, it's not your fault or anything."

My fault? Like I planned this? Right then, crabbiness beat out embarrassment. "I'm glad I have your permission," I said, handing the canteen back to him. "Really!"

"Don't get mad," Ryan pleaded. "I know you're emotional—"

"I am not emotional!" I replied, and then started to laugh, rubbing my eyelids, defeated. "Well, maybe a little."

"Look at the mountains," Ryan suggested with a cautious smile. "Breathe in the Rocky Mountain air. . . . Do you want to get back the fastest way possible, or do you want to avoid all of the suicide trails?"

"Let's go fast," I replied, deciding to be brave for a change, "and please stop staring like that." I didn't need him to keep studying my sweaty, zit-nosed face.

When the trail widened, I guided my horse to the lead, pretty sure the stain wasn't visible as long as I stayed put on the saddle. Ryan followed me up the last suicide trail. A cliff to my right plunged thousands of feet. The pass wrapped tightly around the mountain.

Things couldn't get worse, I decided, proud of myself for acting semi-grown-up.

Then, as it started raining harder, Popeye carried me around a bend and I found myself face-to-face with a huge animal. Supersized. *Enormous*. It looked sort of like a cow, but much larger, with a thicker, woolly neck. It wasn't quite a buffalo.

"Um?" I was too scared to think. "Ryan?"

"He's a beefalo" came Ryan's answer, calm and steady.

Ryan and his horse paused behind Popeye and me. Neither horse had room on the muddy trail to turn around and retreat. The wall of an animal in front of me didn't either.

"He's a *what*?" I asked, not so steady, not so calm.

"Beef-a-lo. Part cow, part buffalo. They've got sweet, lean meat."

And I'd thought broccoflower was a creepy idea. Setting aside the prickly issue of naming an animal after what its meat is called, I fretted that either Beefy or Popeye and I—especially Popeye and I—would be leaving the mountaintop the hard way.

"Trust Popeye," Ryan said. "You'll be all right."

A moment passed, then another. I was too freaked

out to mind my cramps or my headache. I couldn't have cared less that Ryan knew I'd started my period or if he'd spotted the zit. "R–Ryan?" I called, voice wavering.

"Easy," he replied. "Take slow, deep breaths."

My breath came fast. My breath came shallow.

Popeye moved one hoof back, then another. *Clop, clop* on the muddy path. *Clop, clop. Clop, clop . . . clop, clop.* Beefy stayed put.

I petted Popeye's coarse mane, grateful. *Clop, clop . . . clop, clop.* I could hear Ryan's horse walking slowly backward as well. *Clop, clop . . . clop, clop* to safety.

Beefy held his ground, blinking at me.

Where I'd taken the lead, the horses maneuvered into a headfirst retreat. *Clop, clop, clop, clop.* Once we reached the meadow, I began laughing in relief. "Was that supposed to be on the tour?"

"Not exactly." Ryan shook his head and adjusted his hat for the breaking sunlight. "Are you, you know, going to be okay?"

He was talking about my . . . condition, I realized. My period, not my panic attack. "Yeah, no. Um . . ." The stable would be crowded with cowboys, most of them teenagers, probably none of them as understanding as Ryan.

"Come on," he said as the shower tapered off. "We're almost there."

We didn't say anything else until the bustling stable came into view. I wanted to thank him. Despite everything—the heights, the rain, my peeing, the suicide paths, the beefalo, and my period—Ryan had made a worst-case scenario survivable. Somehow, I wasn't even embarrassed anymore. He'd started off as a perfect stranger and ended up a perfect gentleman.

I didn't want his last image of me to be the girl with the retreating red stain.

But before I could begin my speech, Ryan pulled a blanket roll out of one of his saddlebags and handed it over. "Tie this around your waist," he said. "You can keep it."

"I love you," I told him, not completely joking.

"I have four sisters, remember?" Ryan replied. "Rachel, Rebecca, Ronnie, and Reba? You're not the first girl this has ever happened to."

He smiled at me, nice and steady. I grinned back. So, I was a girl, I thought. A woman, almost. So what. If Ryan could deal with it, so could I.

# Living on Chocolate
## Dian Curtis Regan

I lived on Chocolate Circle two months before I realized the sign on the corner referred to me—DEAF CHILD AREA.

I hadn't paid much attention because my eyes always shifted to the other sign—the street sign—and I'd start wondering why anyone would pick such an absurd name.

My first day at Colley Middle School, I wrote on the board that I lived on Chocolate. When I turned around, I could see the class laughing. At first, I thought they were laughing at *me*. I should be used to that by now, but I'm not.

Nexio, one of the other foster kids staying here at the Morenos', caught up with me that first day as I walked home from the bus. He pointed at the Deaf Child sign in a teasing way. "Look, Annie. They put that up because of you."

At least that's what I think he said. I've never been good at reading lips unless people talk as slow as grass grows. I watch their lips and strain my ears. I can hear sounds—but not very well. It's like trying to listen through padded earmuffs.

I'd rather live in the stories in my books than try to talk to people. It's easier.

I came to the Morenos' in Wichita from the Landerses' in Topeka. Mrs. Landers changed her mind about keeping a foster kid. I don't blame her. She didn't choose me. The state dumped me on her.

I used to pretend Mrs. Landers was my mother just because she nudged me out of bed every morning and led me to a bowl of oatmeal. Then one day she up and announced she was getting rid of me. A heart can barely handle that sort of thing.

My real mother got rid of me when I was seven. She took me to day care almost every day—even on weekends, because she had two jobs. She always complained about how much it cost.

Then, when I was in second grade, I came down with an infection so bad, it ruined the nerves in my ears. I was in the hospital for a long time. When I got out, my mother told me, "I can't take care of you anymore."

That's when I started counting on books instead of people.

The social worker who drove me to the Landerses' with my Minnie Mouse suitcase and stuffed walrus tried to explain about welfare and hospital bills, and how no one could locate my father. I was too young to know what she was talking about, but I still remember how she made me watch her lips as she practically shouted the words so they'd sink in.

For five years I tried to forget my real mother and love Mrs. Landers; then she pulled the same rotten trick. She explained her reason a dozen times, then, just to make sure I understood, sent me off with a note that repeated it one more time: "I'm getting out of the foster parent business so I can travel before I get too old. Thank you for understanding. And . . . good luck!"

"Good luck" is something you tell a person who's going off on an adventure—not someone you're shoving out of a home she's lived in almost half her life.

Here in Wichita I might as well be a rock in the garden. The Morenos have four kids of their own, plus five foster kids. It's a zoo. I'm stuck in a bedroom in the musty basement with Tonisha, eleven, and Chell, twelve, like me. They chatter half the night. I catch words and phrases before the lights go out. Topics range from bras to mascara (neither of which Mrs. Moreno will allow yet).

Whenever I try to join the conversation, they gape at me, roll their eyes, and laugh. I know my voice sounds funny; I can't help it. Before the infection ruined my ears, I could talk. But afterward, I forgot how to say things the right way.

So, I live here on Chocolate, waiting for this family to get rid of me, too. Send me down the road to the next Kansas town. This time I know better than to pretend Mrs. Moreno is my mother.

Last night everyone was grabbing for the spatula after she frosted a birthday cake for Nexio. *I* was the one she handed it to.

Yes, I know it was nice of her, but I also know that any day I could find my Minnie Mouse suitcase on the bed, packed, along with my raggedy walrus. I will never get rid of that walrus. I take care of things I love.

The one who talks to me the most is Sol. She's not a foster kid; she's a Moreno. Her name means "sun" in Spanish. She wears a sun choker and a sun toe ring and even a tiny sun tattoo on her bony hip. (She showed me but made me promise not to tell.)

Sol goes to Loomis High while I'm stuck at Colley, where they mainstream me. Not that I don't want to be mainstreamed, but it's lonely in a class of thirty kids who ignore me because I'm different. Because I can't join in on jokes and teasing and whispered gossip.

Back in Topeka I took classes with other hearing-impaired students. We signed to one another, even though the teacher tried to get us to lip read.

Signing is easier, but no one at Colley knows how. I miss my friend Ruby in Topeka. She was born deaf. We e-mail each other every day.

It's a warm Friday night, and I'm sitting on the grass in the Morenos' backyard, waiting for my turn at the computer. When there are nine kids in one family, computer time is allocated in twenty-minute segments. Mrs. Moreno draws names from a Tupperware cup to determine the order.

I hug my knees, groaning quietly so no one on the porch can hear. My stomach has been cramping since noon, and I wonder if I'm coming down with the flu. No one gets the flu in May; it's a winter illness. Why do I always have to be different?

I don't want to tell Mrs. Moreno, because I don't know her well enough to explain about this pain rolling through my stomach.

She is captain of this ship: *"Unload the dishwasher! Napkins on each plate!"* I am a cricket on the deck— not worth noticing, yet in danger of being squished by too many shoes.

Mrs. Moreno hardly ever talks to me. I don't think she's being mean; I think she's too busy. The baby is still in diapers, and she nurses him without even stopping to sit.

I check my watch. Five minutes until my computer time when I can e-mail Ruby. I think I have to go to the bathroom—that's how bad the pain is.

I wait by the bathroom door until Sol comes out. She smiles and asks (slowly, so I will understand), "Are you okay?"

*Oh, great, I even look sick.* I nod and brush past her, locking the door. I feel terrible. A tingly headache pricks my forehead.

Suddenly a warmth surges through me. I think I've wet my pants. "Annie!" I whisper-hiss in disgust even though I cannot hear my own voice. "You're weird enough; don't get weirder."

It's blood.

I gaze at the red stain. The sight of it makes me

sick. Waves of nausea sting my stomach. Blood? At first I'm confused.

I clean myself up and stare into the mirror. My freckles float dark against my pale skin. I wonder what it's like to be blind instead of deaf. Is it better to see a face or hear a voice? I desperately want to know the answer, but the question is way too hard.

It's seven minutes into my computer time, but I can't move. My confusion clears. I know what's happening; I'm not dumb. The nurse at the school in Topeka explained it, but I'm such a poor lip reader, I didn't understand, even after Ruby signed to me, "My sister got her period when she was my age, but I haven't yet. Have you?"

I didn't know what she meant. I felt stupid. The nurse made us ask our questions out loud, which did me no good.

Afterward I read a booklet the nurse gave us. Then I understood the word *period*. I remember feeling amazed to learn about this miserable monthly bleeding business. How could anyone consider such an icky thing normal?

The door latch is jiggling. I place my hand on the wood and feel a vibration. Someone is pounding to get in. Quickly I shove tissue paper into my underpants and wash my hands.

I open the door. Nexio is blathering about . . . what? Needing the bathroom? My lost computer time?

I hurry to the corner of the family room. Tonisha, perched at the computer, gives me a sly smile and shrugs. I take it to mean, "Since you weren't here, I went on without you."

I no longer care, although I hate not getting Ruby's daily message. She's probably wondering what happened to me, and it's not like I can call her on the phone and explain.

I run downstairs to the basement and change into my pajamas. I put on clean underwear and shove half a box of tissues inside. I want to wash the soiled pair in the laundry sink, but there are too many people around. Paula and Ling (the youngest foster kids) are watching a video in plain view of the sink.

I throw the panties into the garbage.

At this rate I'll be totally out of underwear by next weekend.

I am in bed by eight o'clock, reading and hugging my walrus. I've never named him. I worry if I give him a name, someone will take him away. It's better to be anonymous.

In a flash it occurs to me that getting my period

means I can someday have a baby. Suddenly I love that future baby with such a fierceness, I know I will never act like my mother—even if something is terribly wrong with the child. Even if it's like me.

I imagine my real baby, born with tusks and fins, and it makes me hug my walrus with the same fierceness.

I should go ask Mrs. Moreno if I can take a pill for the pain, but then she'd know something is wrong. I don't want her to think I'm a problem.

I want to be an unnamed walrus.

The bedroom light startles me. I brace for Chell's and Tonisha's invasion, but it's Sol. She sits on my bed and signs, "Hello, Annie," to me.

I am pleased to see her "speaking my language."

"What's wrong?" Sol asks slowly. "You're acting strange tonight."

"I act strange every night," I answer, forcing out the words as clearly as I can. She laughs, so I know she understands.

"We need to talk," she says, signing the words I taught her and mouthing the rest. "I just took out the garbage and found something interesting inside."

My heart skitters. I sit up, clutching the bedcovers as if they can hold me safe in this house. I am deciphering only part of what Sol is saying, but I know I've been caught. Will they send me away?

"I asked your roomies," Sol continues, "but they knew nothing about it, so I assume the item in the garbage belongs to you?"

I'm afraid to look at her. "I think I got my first period."

Sol gathers my walrus and me into a hug, then pulls back so I can read her lips. "This is good news, Annie. No need to hide it. Welcome to the Secret Girls' Club."

She laughs at what is probably a goofy look on my face. The thought of belonging to any sort of club thrills me.

"I'll bring you some pads and show you how to use them. Do you need anything else? Advil? Chocolate?"

"Both!" I exclaim, laughing. "But don't tell Mrs. Moreno."

Confusion scatters her tender look. "Why not? You've done nothing wrong. When this happened to me, Mom took me to lunch for a secret celebration. Let's do the same for you tomorrow."

Surprise and relief quell the cramping. I know she's right. I should celebrate. For once I'm just like every other girl.

I start to say this to Sol when the door flies open and Tonisha and Chell tumble in.

"Was it her?" Tonisha blurts. "Annie?"

I am shocked by the look of awe on her face, and how Chell waits wide eyed for me to answer. Waits for me to speak.

"Yes, it's me."

I expect them to laugh at my voice, but they don't. They *ooooh* and *ahhh* instead. Chell even touches my shoulder as if to make sure I'm still human. "This is soooo cool. We're the same age. Maybe *I'll* start soon."

"Me too," Tonisha chirps.

Then they repeat their words to make sure I understand—which I do because they are practically yelling in excitement.

Sol pats me. "Wait here. I'll go get everything you need."

After she leaves, the other two pounce on me with their loud questions: "What's it like? Does it hurt? How do you feel?"

I answer, signing as I speak, in hopes they might pick up a few gestures. They start to imitate the hand movements with such sincerity, it pinches my heart.

Inside, I'm as excited as they are—but mostly

because they're including me. I cannot wait to e-mail this news to Ruby.

My walrus and I settle in to wait for Sol. Tonisha and Chell switch topics (to bras and mascara) but keep facing me and speaking slowly so I can be part of the conversation. I put my book away for the night, grinning, unable to squelch my giddiness.

Sol returns with pads and Advil—and with Mrs. Moreno. My joy melts into panic.

Mrs. Moreno smiles at me. She pretends to applaud, then fusses over how I'm feeling. She's even brought a gift: a Hershey bar.

I feel like crying. A heart can barely handle this sort of thing.

Maybe life on Chocolate won't be so bad.

And maybe it's time I gave this raggedy ol' walrus a name.

# Runaway Sheep

### Florence Johnson Jacob
*As retold by her granddaughter,*
*Kristin Embry Litchman*

**A UTAH FARM, 1902**

"There's two spring lambs missing," said Father when he came in for his noon dinner. "They've probably gone toward the creek. Florence, you and Grace take the wagon and go fetch them home."

The sisters grabbed their sunbonnets and skedaddled out of the house before he could change his mind and send their older sister, Adeline, instead.

"No lollygagging, now," said Father as he boosted them into the battered farm wagon. "Be back before supper time."

"We will."

Florence flapped the reins, and Blackie ambled out of the yard. They passed Adeline, pegging out damp overalls on the clothesline. She made a face at her sisters and they stuck out their tongues in reply, glad for this unexpected holiday from laundry chores. They waved at their brothers in the sheep pen near the barn.

"I'll stand up and look while you drive," said Grace, lurching to her feet and clutching her sister's shoulder for balance. "That'll be faster."

"All right." Florence urged Blackie along the wagon track toward the creek, hoping the lambs hadn't wandered too far away. Down below her belly button, her tummy was feeling vaguely uneasy, as if she had eaten food left out too long in the heat.

The fall sun warmed them, though a brisk wind shoved clouds across the sky. The girls swiveled their heads as they rode, watching everywhere for white patches among the sagebrush. Jackrabbits bounced out of their way, and small rodents skittered out of sight, but they didn't lay eyes on a single sheep the whole three miles to the creek.

By the time they reached the creek, the white clouds were turning gray and filling the sky. With the sun's disappearance, the wind felt chill, and their holiday feeling began to ooze away. Florence had a real tummy ache now, but she said nothing to Grace. They still had to find those lambs.

They left Blackie and the wagon near the creek and set off to search on foot, one upstream and one down. As the sky grew darker, Florence plodded upstream and in a wide circle back toward the wagon. The ache below her belly button was growing stronger, more painful, making it hard to think about sheep. She just wanted to get home to Mama.

Grace hadn't seen the sheep. "Maybe they're dead," she said when Florence met her at the wagon.

"Then we better find their corpses so we can tell Father where they are. I'm not hauling any sheep bodies home." Florence's uneasy innards turned over at the thought.

"Me either. What now?"

"Tie Blackie up the road a ways and look again. Then keep doing it until we've searched as much as we can."

On her fourth search, Florence, who wanted only to curl up under a friendly sagebrush and go straight to sleep, heard a faint shout.

"Found 'em!"

It took her a few moments to realize that Grace was calling about the lost lambs. She gritted her teeth and stumbled toward that faint voice. And in the middle of a clump of sagebrush were the two hefty lambs. They bawled at Grace as she tried to shoo them toward the wagon.

"Push them," said Florence. "*Make* them go."

The girls shoved. They pulled. The sheep took a few steps and stopped, protesting loudly. "I'll bring the wagon here," said Grace.

"All right." It was beginning to rain. Florence sat near a sagebrush to wait, huddling her knees to her chest. The ache felt a little better that way. The lambs turned their backs to the wind, and she envied their woolly coats.

Grace couldn't get the wagon all the way to the lambs, and in the end the girls lugged one, kicking and bleating, to the wagon. The other lamb trotted after them, *baa*ing.

The thunder began as they struggled to lift the first lamb over the wagon's tailgate. The lamb kicked. Lightning flickered.

"Push!" yelled Florence, and Grace pushed with her.

The first lamb was in. Florence grabbed for the second lamb. "Get in and pull, Grace, while I push." She stood the lamb on its hind legs, and Grace reached out for the front legs. But as the second lamb went over the tailgate, the first lamb was climbing out again.

Rain streamed down. Florence couldn't even tell

if she was crying. She felt sick, and scared because she'd never felt sick like this before. She worried over what Father would say if they got back without both sheep.

The lambs bleated and kicked. The girls yanked and shoved. Finally, soaking with rainwater, they heaved both lambs aboard. Florence, clambering up the wagon wheel, slipped and fell to the ground, landing hard on her tailbone.

"You hurt?" called Grace.

"I hurt all over," said Florence. She didn't want to move, but Grace insisted she get into the wagon. Before they could pick up the reins, Blackie, who disliked storms and noisy lambs, started for home at a trot. The wagon jolted over the rough road, tumbling girls and lambs around its wet bed. Florence grabbed for the reins, and Grace lay across both thrashing lambs.

"You keep ahold of those lambs," said Florence. "I don't feel so good." It was all she could do to hang on to the reins all the long wet way home.

Adeline was watching for them through the kitchen window. She came out in the half-dark with a lantern. "Hurry up. I'm not standing out here all night."

Florence and Grace tumbled the lambs over the wagon's side to Father, who shoved them into the pen. "I'll take care of Blackie" was all he said, but they knew that meant he was satisfied with their work.

Adeline held the lantern. Florence climbed backward out of the wagon.

Grace, who had scrambled down before her, saw her sister's skirt in the light. "Florence! You're all bloody in back. Did you hurt yourself when you fell?"

Florence twisted around and tugged her skirt enough to see that yes, indeed, it was red with blood. "Maybe I got cut."

Adeline had seen, too. "Go show Mama right now," she said. Her face had an odd, secret expression, and Florence ran for the house, feeling something trickle down her legs. Was she bleeding to death? Grace and Adeline ran after her.

Mama, stirring gravy at the stove, glanced briefly at her daughters. "You took long enough."

Grace spoke up. "Florence fell, Mama. She's hurt."

Florence couldn't speak. She just turned around so Mama could see her skirt.

Mama laid down the big wooden spoon. "Grace, you go out and help Father." She waited for Grace to leave the room, and went on, "You're not hurt, Florence. Now you know what it's like to be a woman."

"But what happened, Mama?"

"Nothing more than happens to every girl. It's good

this was wash day. There's water and suds left in the washtub for your skirt and petticoat and drawers. You can rinse out your duds in the morning, Florence."

As she talked, Mama pulled a nightgown from the drying rack near the fire. "Adeline, fetch some clean rags from the corner cupboard."

"Mama . . . you never told me—"

"There was no call to tell you anything. I knew you'd find out for yourself soon enough."

"But I—"

"Not now, Florence. Ask your sister after supper."

Numb with shock and fright, Florence let Mama and Adeline bathe her and put on the rags and the nightgown. Then Grace and the boys and Father came in, demanding supper. There wasn't time to sort out what had happened.

That night in their bedroom, Adeline whispered a scrambled explanation to her astonished sisters.

"Bleeding every month?" asked Grace. "Will it happen to me, too?"

"Of course, silly," said Adeline. "Mama never told me, either, Florence. But it's not so bad. You get used to it after a while."

Florence climbed into bed and pulled up the quilt.

"Next time *you* go for the sheep," was all she said.

# Making Do

Rita Williams-Garcia

Ma had a way of treating the most exciting, unusual events like they were perfectly normal. When Aretha Franklin's tour bus stopped in Howard on its way to Atlanta, Ma said, "Lucy Ray, go down to the depot and ask Miss Franklin to supper." It was in that same factual manner she said, "Your daddy's bringing home a Freedom Rider. Clean out a drawer."

Her name was Dorinda Adams, which seemed pretty ordinary for a Freedom Rider. "Social activist" was what she called herself when Pa brought her up to my room. In spite of some folks calling our guest a troublemaker, Ma either referred to her as a Freedom Rider or a college girl. I found that to be funny, because standing shoulder to shoulder to Pa and towering over Ma in her square-toed flats, Dorinda Adams was hardly a girl. Not to mention that her round, woolly Afro bush gave her a slight advantage over Daddy. By the way he looked up to her and cocked his head short of a *whoooeee*, I knew Daddy was amazed by her.

Dorinda was a long way from Chicago, her hometown, and even farther from Boston, which is where she went to law school. She was one of many college students who had piled into cars or taken Greyhounds down South to make sure colored people were registered to vote in the '68 election. As dangerous as that was, I found Dorinda's being a law student even more remarkable than her being so tall or a social activist. I'd seen colored women teachers, one medical doctor, a couple of truck drivers, and some singers on TV. But as far as I knew, there were no colored women lawyers or law students. I could well be sharing my room and dresser drawer with the first one.

My eyes never left her army-style duffel bag once she drew it open and began to unpack. I lay on my belly just a-gawking, hoping to see some far-out clothes or even a forbidden item that a college student might have, like a marijuana cigarette. After I saw her unpack one plain dress, two pairs of bell-bottoms, three blouses, one pair of stockings, one pair of socks, one brassiere, four pairs of panties—the plain old cotton kind I wore—some fountain pens, and a mess of Voting Rights Act papers, I was thoroughly disappointed.

"Is that all you have?"

"It's all I need," she replied. "You have to travel light for the cause."

For the cause. She sounded mysterious and important. Still, I expected more to come out of that duffel bag. My disappointment amused her somewhat, because she smiled, which was hard to catch, being that she wore round, tinted granny glasses and her smile was in her eyes.

I was going to leave Dorinda in peace to get settled, but then she took out her last two items from the bottom of the duffel bag, and I stayed put. The first was a small denim drawstring bag and the other was a box of Sani-Pads. Although I personally didn't use Sani-Pads—or any other brand—I had seen that powder blue box in stores and in girls' lockers. My curiosity now darted to the drawstring bag. "What's that for?" I was being nosy, but I felt I had a right.

She smiled in her eyes again and said, "It's my emergency kit." She took two sanitary napkins from the box, folded them, and then stuffed them into the drawstring bag, which she tied to her belt loop. "I always carry a roll of dimes for the telephone, a toothbrush, and two napkins during that time of the month."

Before I could ask why, she added, "I can be arrested at any time."

I picked up the box of Sani-Pads. "Have you ever been arrested?"

She shook her head no, and I thought, Now that's the way to have an Afro. Dorinda's Afro was perfectly round and wouldn't have budged if the wind was wicked. Janet Minkins tried to help me style an Afro, but it wouldn't take, on account of Ma's Indian blood. I just didn't inherit enough of Pa's thick, kinky hair. Naps is what he called them.

"I haven't been arrested, but I've traveled on buses for hours without a pad change. Toilet paper just doesn't cut it. These," she said, squeezing the bulk in her drawstring bag, "are a must."

I tossed the Sani-Pads box up and caught it a couple times, like it was a softball. Then I stopped, seeing how I was annoying her.

"We don't use those," I said, putting the box back on the bed.

It made her no-never-mind. But just to clarify

things I said, "Throw-away napkins aren't good for the earth."

"Then what do you use?" she asked.

"Cloth," I said. "Torn-up bed sheets. Pa's old shirts. We just make do."

"Are you serious?" It was as though I had said the unthinkable. I never pictured another colored person making that face at me. There she was, shocked by the ordinary, giving me a look that my mind had reserved for white people.

It was all because of Ma. Ma didn't believe in disposable. She'd shake her head whenever commercials on TV boasted how disposable their goods were and how they freed the housewife from her life of drudgery. Disposable diapers, handy rags, paper plates, plastic cups, and scribbled-on writing paper got her goat. I wasn't even allowed to ball up a composition and try again on a fresh sheet. Instead, I was to squeeze my brain until I achieved order and perfection, not to mention correct spelling. No matter how hard I pleaded for a fresh sheet of paper, Ma would say, "No, Sister. Somewhere there's mountains of disposable goods touching the sky, pushing out into all that's brown, green, and blue."

We had so little garbage it was a shame to come and collect it.

Ma used to pack up tin cans, wash them out, and send them back to Del Monte or Libby with a note: "Perfectly good tin. Reuse them."

Reusing and making do was normal in our house. When you grow up reusing, you don't know any different. In fact, I'd actually looked forward to getting my first ripped cloth napkins. No one ever talked about what they used, but by sixth and seventh grade, we were all happily reporting to one another that we had "our friend." By the eighth grade, it was nothing special, although Miss Fowler, our gym teacher, always let girls sit on the sidelines when they complained of headaches and unmentionable discomforts. That was exactly what they said: "Miss Fowler, I'm having unmentionable discomfort," and she'd mark them present and have them sit while the rest of us did our calisthenics.

I wasn't allowed to have any unmentionable discomforts. When I was twelve, Ma took me aside and said, "Now, Sister"—she called me that because she had four brothers and no sister—"you're fittin' to get your blood flowing. It's nothing to worry about. Even Penny and Sophie"—our female pigs—"bleed. Don't go making it more'n what it is."

Ma was right for the most part. It wasn't a big

deal, except one day a white classmate, Margaret Evans, had asked me for an extra napkin. She would die if she had to walk all the way to the nurse's office. For the first time, I was ashamed of my cloth napkins. I snapped my fingers, faking regret, and said, "Darn it if I didn't use the last one this morning." Margaret was genuinely horrified for me and said, "We have three more hours of school. What will you do?" I offered to go to the nurse's office for the both of us.

I hurried back with two napkins inside a clasped manila envelope. One for her, one for me. My napkin was strictly for school use. I couldn't dispose of it at home. There was no newspaper to wrap it in, and our garbage was so small that it would be discovered, especially if Penny or Sophie got to it. I kept my one disposable napkin in my locker for a future emergency, such as this. I even practiced offering it: "Here you go, Margaret. Anytime."

Dorinda Adams was thoroughly amazed about how we made do in our house. It was as though I had told her we sat around the table eating dirt. "So let me get this straight," she said, pushing down her granny glasses. "You use cloth? Only cloth?"

"That's right." Now I sounded like Ma. Factual.

"And what do you do when they're used?" She was practicing her lawyering skills, cross-examining me like the district attorney on *Perry Mason*. I don't recall ever seeing a colored female in Perry Mason's TV courtroom, and certainly not arguing any case.

"First we soak them in bleach. Then we scrub them with borax soap, rinse them, and dry them on the line."

"Sooner or later you have to throw them away, don't you?"

"We burn them," I answered.

"Burn them? I've never heard of that. Burning sanitary napkins."

"Blood and cotton. Nature going back to nature." That was how Ma explained it to me.

"Well, I hope you all don't expect *me* to make do."

"Ma'll let you slide 'cause you're our guest. I'm just telling you what's normal round here."

After supper we sat in front of the television to watch the evening news. They always started with the war, which we listened to intently because both my brothers, Harold and Lem, were in Danang. From the war the news always switched to the White House, then to what was happening in the bigger cities across the country, and finally to our local news. We were watching troops of Black Panthers with rifles marching through the streets of Oakland, then San Francisco, and then Harlem. The news cameras made it seem like there were Black Panthers on every street corner. In spite of the national report, there were no Black Panthers toting rifles and making fists in Howard or anywhere nearby.

Dorinda had just rejoined us after excusing herself to "freshen up." She was drawn right in to the TV set, drinking in every word dictated by the Panther spokesman in his leather jacket and black beret. Ma wasn't too impressed with the Black Panthers. I think it was because Harold and Lem were wading through the rice paddies while the Panthers were playing soldier.

"It ain't nothing to carrying a rifle," Ma said of the Panthers. "Lucy Ray can shoot the eyes off a rutting buck."

I was a pretty good shot, but not all that good like Ma said. It was a rare moment when she let her pride jump out like that. I was embarrassed.

"The Panther presence in urban neighborhoods makes an important statement," Dorinda spoke up. She had been mindlessly playing with her emergency kit, still strung to her belt loop. Poor thing. She really couldn't be without it, although I couldn't imagine Sheriff Bradley kicking down our door to haul her away. "Those brothers and sisters are willing to defend their people and die for what they believe in."

"Die?" Ma said. "Die? Those boys aren't fittin' to die. They're strutting in front of my TV, showing their rifle and their handshake. If you fittin' to die, you don't pose in front of the news cameras."

Back when Ma was a girl, Ma, Grampa, and my uncles spent many a night on the porch with rifles, waiting for the Klan. Grampa was Creek and Grandma was colored. All my uncles were colored enough to get strung up. They did that a lot when my mother was a little girl. Strung up colored.

Ma said, "Dorinda. You coming here to educate folks about voting is making a statement."

Pa nodded his support to Ma's words, but I could see Dorinda thought Ma was being funny. I read her eyes behind the glasses.

Ma was a quick reader herself. She stamped her foot and said, "No, no. It's important. In the last election at least fifty colored went to the courthouse to vote. Only twelve of us passed the test. Me, Pa, the schoolteachers, Reverend Sikes, Mrs. Reverend,

Dr. Minkins. And there's worse things been done than reading and history tests to keep coloreds from voting."

Dorinda winced when Ma said "colored," but that's what we said. Colored.

"LBJ might have signed the Voting Rights Act of '65," Pa jumped in, "but to some of these good old boys, it's business as usual." Pa voted for President Johnson. That was no secret. Not with that "All the way with LBJ" sticker plastered on the back of his pick-up truck.

"Mark my words," Ma told Dorinda. "You are more of a threat to them good old boys than them Panthers in leather jackets. You're bringing the law to the people. Educating them. Now that's something dangerous."

"Mind you, Dorinda, girl," my daddy said, "they'll be watching you."

Sunday morning Dorinda was already rolling up her clothes to put back into her duffel bag. She had only six weeks to register voters, and she had a map of churches with red Xs to spread her gospel, which I was anxious to hear. After today's church service, she was leaving Howard and heading down to Florida. She said she had her work cut out for her down in the swamps.

Dorinda laid out her tools on the bed: a stack of Voting Rights Act leaflets, some voters' registration forms, and a handful of fountain pens. She took a sanitary napkin from the Sani-Pads box and excused herself. While she was in the bathroom, I picked up the powder blue box and read the words printed on it: "Soft and absorbent. Clean and confidential." I put the box in her duffel bag. Sometimes you yearn for something normal. Something as simple as a box of sanitary napkins.

Dorinda came back to the bedroom and tugged the bodice darts on her one good dress, the kind that never needed ironing, and preened before the mirror, patting her Afro. "I'm not a dress wearer," she said. "This is what I wear to churches for voters' registration. Folks are more receptive if I look a certain way. Anything for the cause."

Ma was a definite dress wearer, but it didn't make her normal among other women. It made her unusual. If she was fishing, pulling up turnips, or smoking a ham, Ma was in one of her A-line, button-down, cotton dresses, whereas I only wore dresses to school and church. When I asked Ma why she never wore pants, not even to fish in, she said, "For the freedom, Sister! Feel that air." Lucky

I wasn't the blushing sort.

"Girls! Let's get a move on," Ma called. I think Ma was more anxious for this day than Dorinda.

We scurried. Dorinda grabbed her leaflets and forms, and I took the fountain pens. As we were dashing out of the house, I felt this charge of nerves or panic, like I had forgotten something. When I got to the car, I realized it had to be my Bible. You couldn't follow Reverend Sikes without a Bible, and I had my chapter corners turned just right, so I ran back to my room and got it. Even as we were driving on down to the church, that panicky feeling hadn't completely left me. Maybe I was nervous for Dorinda, having to speak before all those people, knowing she had unmentionable discomforts and needed to "freshen up" every two hours.

As soon as the church service was over, we went down to the basement, which was our meeting place. Reverend Sikes introduced Dorinda as a third-year law student and an intern for the federal government, which drew "ahs" from the folks who came to hear her, in spite of the talk spreading that she was a Black Panther and a communist. That talk had come from Miss Wanda's World of Beauty. Miss Wanda had recently ordered twelve dozen jars of cream relaxer from Chicago. She looked upon the Afro, sported by Dorinda and the Black Panthers, as nothing but trouble.

Dorinda took her place and began to speak. Even in her pea green dress, she looked like a mighty figure, not at all as she had hoped to come off: like a regular girl, just one of the folks. One thing was for sure. Dorinda proved to be a rousing speaker who knew her way around a Baptist audience. When she spoke, the audience—mostly Ma—spoke back. Dorinda could have been in her dorm room, studying, curled up with tea and a hot-water bottle, but she was here in Howard. I knew Ma insisted that we take her in for my benefit. That kind of company rubs off on you.

"Three years ago, President Lyndon Baines Johnson signed the Voting Rights Act of 1965. Do you know what that means to all Americans?"

Dorinda detailed the what, how, and why of the Voting Rights Act. She even made heroes of those who had failed to pass those illegal reading and history tests in the last elections. But now was the hard part. Trying to keep folks vigilant about their rights.

"You hear that?" Ma called out. "Our right to vote is guaranteed."

"If you *do not* understand your rights, if you *do not*

register," Dorinda preached, her fist pounding on the "do nots," "if you *do not* show up at the polls, if you *do not* put the right president in office, you will wake up one day and think it's 1940."

The congregation went wild. Dorinda paused to let their reaction subside. In all of the commotion, no one had noticed that Sheriff Bradley had entered our meeting, until he was standing there, broader than a man his height ought to be. Reminded you of a football player, the kind that blocked two at a time.

He had come for Dorinda.

Reverend Sikes said, "This is holy ground. You cannot arrest anyone in here."

"I don't see anything holy going on," Sheriff Bradley said. "I don't see no praying and singing." He led Dorinda away. She didn't even resist, as if she had been expecting him.

Ma wasn't ready to give up her guest speaker so easily. She called after Sheriff Bradley, "What are the charges?"

"Disturbing the peace. Illegal assembly. Spreading communist propaganda." He might as well have been reading his answer.

"Horse apples," Ma said. "Since when is a church meeting an illegal assembly?"

Pa and Mrs. Reverend tried to hold her back. Pa

knew the sheriff wasn't going to put up with Ma but for so long. Even I was afraid for her.

We all followed them out to the patrol car. Dorinda rose her fist in the air and shouted, "Don't give up your right to vote! Don't give up your right to vote!"

Sheriff Bradley reached up, put his hand on Dorinda's round Afro, and squashed her down into the backseat.

Ma diverted her attention from Dorinda and started handing out the voting papers. "You heard her. There's an election coming. If you're a citizen and twenty-one, you can vote. It's as simple as that."

Folks were still standing around with their mouths open, talking about the sheriff hauling away the law student from Chicago. When Ma tried to put a pamphlet in their hands, folks suddenly had Sunday dinners to prepare. The only ones who'd take the papers were the heroes who regularly came out to the courthouse each election year and tried to vote.

I don't know what disappointed Ma most— Dorinda not being able to finish delivering her message, the people dispersing like chickens, or being left with all of those papers that no one wanted. Some papers had even flown out of Ma's hand. Of course I had to go run and gather them up.

"What're they going to do to Dorinda?" I asked. "Keep her in jail?"

"Naw," Pa said. "They won't hold her long. They'll just put her on the next bus out, then make sure she stays on it."

It didn't seem right that we were having our dinner and our guest was in jail. Sure, Dorinda knew that she could be arrested, but that was why she was prepared. Then I realized what I had known all along in the pit of my stomach. Dorinda had left for church without her emergency kit.

"We're bringing her her stuff, aren't we?"

Ma said we'd see Dorinda off in the morning. Pa said the bus would get in around eleven. I knew she couldn't wait until eleven. She'd be miserable. They didn't have Sani-Pads at the jail. We didn't have any women sheriffs or women lawbreakers, as far as I knew.

I didn't think I could get out of the house with a box of Sani-Pads, so I took the drawstring bag, which had been pushed down into the bottom of Dorinda's duffel bag.

"Lucy Ray, it's too late to be going out," Ma said.

"I know, Ma," I called, walking away with my back to her. There was no winning an argument if I faced her. I had to keep walking if I intended to leave the house. "I'll be back before dark." Then I ran until I got to Janet Minkins's house, where I borrowed her bike to ride the rest of the way. It was a little more than a mile, which was nothing to pedal. I just wanted to get there and give Dorinda her emergency kit. I thought, Anything for the cause!

The sheriff's office was pretty small. It consisted of a desk with a phone, a filing cabinet, and some chairs. Down the hall were two jail cells. I had been inside only once, for a school field trip. The only thing I could remember about it was that the toilets in the cells weren't at all private.

"What you have there?" Sheriff Bradley asked. He was between being amused and being official.

"It's for Dorinda Adams," I said.

He took the drawstring bag and said, "I'll have a look first." He pulled open the bag and dumped everything on his desk. The roll of dimes tore open and dimes spilled everywhere. Next, he took Dorinda's toothbrush, as if he had never seen one before, and pushed his thumb in the bristles, making sure she'd never want to use it. Then he took one of the Sani-Pads.

"That's for females," I said.

"I still have to see it. Never know what can be

hiding in one of these. A file, or a weapon or something."

I could see why Ma treated him with no respect. He was just simple. Pure-T simple. He went on to demonstrate this by tearing the napkins apart. When he was through, he said, "You can see the prisoner. You get five minutes."

I knew he came up with that one on the spot.

Dorinda was curled up on the cot, probably nursing her discomforts as best as she could. Luckily for her, she didn't have to share the cell.

Sheriff Bradley wouldn't open the cell door. I had to stand up to the bars and talk.

"Are you okay?"

I felt I was letting her down when I gave her the denim bag, but she started to laugh, seeing those Sani-Pads all torn up.

"I'm fine," she said. "But now I feel much better."

"I was worried for you, having your friend and all," I whispered. I wouldn't be surprised if Sheriff Bradley was listening.

"There was nothing to worry about," Dorinda said, showing her confidence. "I took a page from your book, Lucy Ray." She gathered up the torn edge of the bed sheet, which was tucked beneath the cot's mattress. Her smile broke through her eyes, tinted granny glasses and all. "I made do."

# You Are a Señorita

Carmen T. Bernier-Grand

I tossed the small rubber ball into the air. As soon as it bounced on the yellow tile floor of our living room, I swooped up five jacks. I didn't move or touch the others, and I caught the ball in midair! I was now ahead of Lulú. But then Mami came in, a bag from the Puerto Rico Drugstore hanging from her arm.

"Lulú, *mijita*," she told my sister. "Please, close those legs." We had our legs spread out into *V*s, forming a perfect diamond for the jacks shining in the middle.

Lulú obeyed, kneeling and sitting on her legs. I kept mine in a *V*, waiting for Mami to tell me to close them. But she put her hand on Lulú's head.

"Come, *corazón mío*, I brought a booklet I want you to read."

Lulú sprang up.

"What about me?" I asked.

Mami, wearing a fashionable, ankle-length skirt, leaned over and touched my cheek. "Carlotita, *mi chiquita,* you won't need this booklet for a year or so."

"Why not?" I asked, peeking inside the bag still hanging from Mami's arm. It had two Kotex boxes. I knew what was inside! Pads of cotton wrapped with gauze. Mami kept those in the bathroom, along with other emergency things.

"Because you're too young," she answered.

"I'm just a year younger than Lulú."

"A year and a half," Lulú said, looking at me over her shoulder. She followed Mami to our bedroom.

"A year, four months, and two days!" I shouted, throwing the ball and the five jacks I'd kept squeezed in my hand. The ball rolled away, but I caught it and hit the jacks—over and over.

Then I picked them up and headed to *my* bedroom, because it wasn't just her bedroom but mine, too.

"Keep it private," I overheard Mami saying. "And

learn it well, so you can help your sister when her time comes."

On her way out of the bedroom, she spotted me and turned me around. "Give Lulú privacy."

So I couldn't go into my own bedroom.

When Lulú got out, I went in and tried to find the booklet. She had hidden it well. It wasn't under her mattress or in her underwear drawer.

But that evening she was reading it in bed, right in my face. I couldn't keep my eyes off the cover. It had a girl wearing *mahones,* tight blue jeans with the cuffs rolled up. The girl had her hair in braids and was looking at herself in a mirror. But the mirror image showed her as a young lady wearing *colorete* on her cheeks, lipstick on her lips, and her hair down. So pretty!

*Ya eres señorita* was the title of the booklet.

"You can't be a *señorita* yet," I said.

Lulú, who had been lying on her stomach with her feet in the air, rolled over and lay on her back. She placed the booklet on top of the two dumb bumps growing on her chest. "Why do you say that?"

"You're only eleven."

"Carlotita, an eleven-year-old can be a *señorita*."

"Unh-unh," I argued.

Lulú slid the booklet down from her body to the chenille bedspread that was just like mine, because Mami had always kept us together by giving us the same things—until now.

Lulú sat up, her hand still on the booklet, and looked into my eyes.

"To be a *señorita*," I said before she could open her mouth, "you have to be fifteen, and then you can wear lipstick like that girl." I pointed at the booklet and that made Lulú sit on it. "And then you can dance with boys at your *quinceañera* birthday party!"

I could hardly wait to be fifteen and a *señorita*! I wanted to go to dances, dance with boys—

"Carlotita." Lulú interrupted my daydreaming. "There's more to being a *señorita* than wearing a gown."

"But I want a gown!"

"Carlotita, you're not listening." She put her feet on my bed. Her second toe was longer than the others, a sign of a bossy person. "There's more to it," she repeated.

"Like what?" I asked, thinking she'd say something about breasts, or boys.

A corkscrew curl swung side to side on Lulú's forehead. "Like Doña Rosa," she said.

"Doña Rosa? Mami's friend with the mustache?"

"No!" Lulú pushed her curl back, but it came down. "Our monthly visitor."

"Who? Who comes to our house every month?"

"¡Ay, Carlotita!" She waved me off. "You don't know anything."

"Well, tell me."

"I wish I could, but obviously you haven't heard about it, and Mami doesn't want me to tell you yet."

I couldn't believe this. We'd never kept secrets from each other. We'd always been close. We went everywhere together. We even dressed alike. People asked us if we were twins. And now this! All because of that stupid *Ya eres señorita* booklet.

Was Lulú really a *señorita*? Was she leaving me behind? I touched my breasts. They were puffy. But Lulú's were bigger. She *was* leaving me behind!

I wouldn't allow it. I had to catch up.

But how?

The next day the "how" became more difficult.

Mami took us back-to-school shopping. At the New York Department Store in San Juan, we chose the same kind of notebooks, with maps of Puerto Rico on the front cover. We bought white erasers because Lulú said the pink kind was for little girls. We chose moccasins with slots to put coins in. We even bought the same kind of panties, seven—a day of the week in English embroidered on each.

But then Mami got bras for Lulú.

"What about me?" I asked.

"You don't need one yet," Mami said.

"I do! I do!" I said, sticking out my chest.

Mami shushed me. She didn't buy me any.

As soon as we got home and Lulú had left the bedroom, I tried on one of hers. My breasts looked pointy big.

"What are you doing?"

Lulú stood in the doorway!

"It . . . it fits me," I said.

"Not really. Watch this." She poked her fingers into the cups. Pop! One cup came back out, but the other stayed in like a punched ball. "See? You're not ready yet."

Okay. Lulú probably filled up a bra better than I could. But she didn't behave like a *señorita* all the time.

A few days later she tied spoons and cans to the back of our old tricycle. I sat on the trike's seat. She stood on the trike's back step, placed her hands on the handles, and pushed the trike so fast that the acerola trees in our backyard seemed to be running.

"Honk! Honk!" she called.

*Clank, clank, clank* went the spoons and cans in back.

"Tra–la–la–laa, tra–la–la–laa!" I sang because this was supposed to be a wedding.

"Honk! Honk!" *Clank, clank, clank!* "Tra–la–la–laa!"

"What's going on?" Mami asked, coming out.

And then all I could see was the concrete fence coming toward me. *AKANGANA!* The tricycle crashed.

I laughed, although Lulú's body weight was pressing down my back. Blood dripped on the trike's handle. Was I hurt? Another drop. I looked up. Lulú's chin had hit the top of the fence, and it was bleeding.

She stood up and placed her hand on her chin. "Ah–ah–ah!" Blood dripped through her fingers.

"Let me see," Mami said, and then rushed her to the bathroom. "Carlotita, get me bandages."

I got a Kotex pad and gave it to Mami.

"Look," she told Lulú.

Lulú, tears still on her cheeks, laughed.

"What's wrong?" I asked.

"This is for Doña Rosa," Lulú said.

"How would I know when you don't tell me who Doña Rosa is?"

"Don't worry," Mami said, as if trying to change the subject. "It works. Lulú, put pressure on that wound. I'll get my purse. I think you need stitches."

"I'm not going to the hospital with this pad on my chin."

"Take an old towel," Mami said.

In the hospital Lulú got five stitches, plastic threads sticking out. She screamed and screamed. I didn't want stitches—ever.

But when I went to the bathroom a few nights later, I found blood on my panties. I'd hurt myself, too! Badly. I probably needed stitches. I couldn't sleep. How could I tell Mami that I'd hurt myself down there? Needed stitches down there? No way. This wound would have to heal itself.

In the middle of the night, I went to the bathroom to check. What a relief! The bleeding had stopped. But when I sat on the toilet the next morning, blood came out. The wound was inside me!

"Mamiii!"

She came in, took one look, and covered her mouth with her hand. Oh no. This was bad. Mami was crying. Maybe I needed surgery. Maybe I was dying.

Then Lulú came in. "Doña Rosa?" she asked stiffly, because of the bandage on her chin.

Mami nodded.

"But her chest is almost flat!"

"I know." Mami was now tying up a Kotex pad to

a white elastic belt. "She surprised me, too."

"Not fair!" Lulú made a face and left the bathroom.

"Am I dying?" I asked.

"No, *mijita*." Mami made me stand so I could put on the belt with a pad. "You're just a *señorita* now."

"A what?"

"A *señorita*, silly," Lulú said, coming back in. She slapped the *Ya eres señorita* booklet into my hands and pointed at my panties. "That's what it takes to be a *señorita*. This is what we call Doña Rosa, *el periodo, menstruación*."

"Ah," I said. I'd overheard Mami saying those last two words to her friend, the real Doña Rosa, the Doña Rosa with the mustache.

But . . . it took blood to be a *señorita*? Not pretty. Not pretty at all.

"Do you do this, too?" I asked Lulú. "I've never seen you wearing a Doña Rosa pad."

She shook her head.

"So what do you do?"

"Carlotita." Mami was washing my panties. "Lulú is not a *señorita* yet."

"She's not?"

Lulú got teary. "And I am older than you. You're lucky!"

Why did she want this?

Still, I didn't want to go through it alone. "I want Lulú to be a *señorita* with me."

"That's nice of you to say," Mami said. "But it doesn't go that way. When it happens, it happens. Read the booklet, *mi amor,* okay?"

I did. The last page showed the young lady wearing a beautiful gown. But Lulú was right. This wasn't about gowns. It was about pads that made me walk like a duck. It was about cramps. It was about not sitting with my legs in a *V* because I had to behave like a *señorita.*

Lulú knew all this. But when I tried to tell her how it really felt, she wouldn't listen. "I don't care," she said. "I don't want to be a *señorita* anymore."

So, on top of everything else, I felt lonely. I did have Mami. But she'd gone through her first period ages ago, and she couldn't quite remember how it had felt.

"*Mi amor,* all that is in the booklet," she said when I asked her too many questions.

I counted twenty-eight days since that fateful day, and my second period came right on time. The sadness, the cramps, the bleeding, the loneliness returned.

One of those mornings, I woke up before Lulú.

Was that blood?

Blood on Lulú's bed?

"Lulú," I whispered, waking her. "I think you're a *señorita*."

She sat. Saw the blood. Giggled. "*¡Ay, sí,* I am!"

I clapped my hands against hers.

She interlocked her fingers with mine. "Cou . . . could you help me?"

"Sure," I said.

We didn't tell Mami right away. Instead we went into the bathroom, where I showed Lulú how to tie the pad to the belt. We were whispering. We were giggling. We were sisters again.

# The Gift

Uma Krishnaswami

*DELHI, INDIA: 1947*

The newspapers had a name for what happened to India. They called it "partition." At summer's end the map of the country was ripped apart. India and Pakistan, two nations newly independent of British rule, were born. And Lakshmi's best friend, Fauzia, went away. "We've been partitioned, too," said Lakshmi. It was true. One day Fauzia had been in school with Lakshmi; the next day she was gone. Her family had joined millions of others making their way to new homelands—Hindus moving to India, Muslims to Pakistan.

"Why, Amma?" Lakshmi appealed to her mother. "Why couldn't she even tell me?"

"Fauzia's family felt it best to leave quickly."

Lakshmi's *amma* busied herself with piles of laundry. "Her brother came by yesterday to return some books. He brought—"

But Lakshmi, not waiting to hear what he'd brought, cried, "He did? You knew? You didn't tell me!"

Amma sighed. "They wanted me to keep it quiet. You've heard the news reports of attacks on refugees. These are hard times." She counted buttons on the clothes as she talked, so she could tell the washerman, "Twenty-two buttons, mind you don't break them!"

Buttons, thought Lakshmi, at a time like this, when the country's falling apart? What's the use of counting buttons?

Partition made terrible things happen. People fought in the streets over whether they prayed on Tuesdays or Fridays, what sort of clothes they wore, or what they called their god. The news was full of stories of Muslims killing Hindus, Hindus killing Muslims, neighbors turning upon neighbors. Partition made families like Fauzia's leave secretly, with no good-byes.

Fauzia gone? It was hard to imagine. No more giggling together. No more stealing marbles from Fauzia's brothers, making Lakshmi's mother say, "You two, stop it! Behave like young ladies, not like tomboys playing marbles!" Now Fauzia's family had left to find a new home in the new country, Pakistan, whose name rang out every day over the radio.

And then there was the man. Lakshmi wondered how long he'd been in the ditch outside the house before they heard him. It was the same ditch she and Fauzia had spent so many hours jumping across, back and forth, back and forth, daring each other to fall in but never falling.

The sound of the man's moans carried to the house, a sound to chill the bones. Lakshmi's father and old Somayya the cook went outside to see who was there. The man uttered another wild and desperate cry, as if gathering his voice for one last wail. Amma gripped the doorknob, her face as closed as the borders between India and Pakistan. "Vasudeva," she murmured, calling on the Hindu god to whom they lit oil lamps at the start of every day, "what have you let them do to that poor soul?"

Old Somayya picked up the man like a baby and carried him to the porch.

"I'll ring Dr. Basu." Lakshmi's father picked up the telephone. Dr. Basu was the family doctor. He would know what to do.

"Appa, who is he? What's the matter with him?

Appa?" Lakshmi's father—her usually cheerful *appa*—seemed not to hear her. He listened now for the operator's voice. He shook the receiver. He shook it again. Then he hung it up on its brass hook. The phone lines were down. "We'll do the best we can," said Appa. But Lakshmi had never seen such a look on his face before. Fear was there, and something else—a terrible defeat.

With a quaking stomach, Lakshmi held splints and watched as her parents tied bandages and the cook brought food and water. "It's all right," they said to the man. "You are safe here." For a moment, in comforting him, their faces calmed and grew gentle.

The man clutched with gratitude the pillow and sheet they gave him. Soon his moans faded to tired snores, and he slept on the bare floor of the trellised porch. In the morning, when they awoke, he was gone, leaving sheet and pillow tidily in a corner.

Lakshmi fancied that somewhere between sleeping and waking, she had heard a murmur of *"Khuda hafiz"* from out there—a Muslim good-bye: God go with you. In these days of blood, it was rumored, how you said hello and good-bye could save or end your life.

Blood! In the morning there was a different kind of blood. It demanded that Lakshmi pay attention to her body. "Amma, I'm bleeding," she said.

"Oh, my dear," said Lakshmi's mother, stopping short in the morning task of pulling curtains open. She looked at Lakshmi as if she were seeing her for the first time in days, as if she were memorizing the lines of her face. "Oh, my dear," she said, "I have been so distracted by all this madness around us, I've had no time for you. You're growing up! This happens to all young girls when they grow up."

"I know, Amma," said Lakshmi. "It happened to Fauzia last month."

Amma shook her head in disapproval. "You girls. Nothing better to talk about?" But she smiled, a rare thing these days. She pulled soft cloth out from the drawer under the bed. She explained how Lakshmi should use it, wash it, hang it separately from the other clothing on the line. "If things were normal, we'd celebrate this, invite friends, buy you new clothes. But we can't do anything now." They sat in silence for a moment, thinking about how violence and fear can overshadow such a thing as a girl growing to be a woman.

"You have become *dooram*," said Amma, using the Tamil word for a woman in her period. Lakshmi had heard the term before, usually to explain why this or that friend of her mother's couldn't go to the temple with them. *Dooram* meant, literally, far away. "It's a time for women to rest," said Amma. "A time not to work, to be apart from the everyday world. In the old days they'd make the women sit by themselves in a separate room, resting, eating special food. And you can't go to a temple when you're bleeding."

All day long Lakshmi marveled at the whole new world her body had entered—a grown-up universe with its own rules and habits. But Amma looked sad. "It's our custom to get girls new bangles when they come of age," she said. "With everything that's going on now, I can't even do that for you."

Lakshmi thought with a pang of Fauzia, to whom she couldn't now say, "Guess what? What's my news? Three guesses!"

"Wait a minute!" Amma tapped her forehead impatiently as if she'd just remembered something. She went into the bedroom and returned with a small red box. "I forgot all about this—I'm sorry." She slipped a silver bracelet out of the box and onto Lakshmi's wrist. "Fauzia left it for you. She wanted you to have it."

Fauzia! Lakshmi ran a finger over the bracelet. It was a little trellis of leaves and flowers, hammered into a delicate circle. She'd seen it often on Fauzia's thin brown wrist.

"No new bangles," said Amma, "but Fauzia's bracelet will do."

"Are they all right, Fauzia's family?" Lakshmi forgot the blood—her own, and the kind spilled in hatred across both sides of a newly made border. She forgot her insides that now ached gently.

Her mother nodded. "They should be. They left before the trouble really started, before the borders were sealed."

"Will she write to me?"

"I don't know," said Amma. "I don't know." The look came back, that careful, closed look. Lakshmi caught her mother's hand in a sudden burst of needing to touch her.

"*Khuda hafiz,*" the man had said. Or had he? Perhaps the words were from a dream.

Perhaps it was Fauzia who had said them.

## POONA, INDIA: 1968

The June Vani turned twelve she thought she was going to die. First she thought she must have hurt herself without knowing it, possibly when she was clambering down from the banyan tree. She'd been in a hurry, as usual. She must have hurt herself, because why else was there blood all over her underpants and skirt and even on her legs? But she didn't mention it to anyone. She just changed into another skirt and washed the first. She hung it out to dry with everyone else's clothes, on the line stretching from the tamarind tree to the house.

"Did I wash that skirt this morning?"

Old Bai scratched her head when she saw the skirt hanging on the line. Bai had been household help, baby-sitter, and laundress since before Vani could remember. "Maybe I did," said Bai. "My memory is fading."

In the morning there was the blood again, and this time Vani knew she was in for a slow and painful death. She felt dizzy thinking of it, and she felt a bit sick. Her body hurt in a way it never had before. She wished she'd spent less time up in the banyan tree. She wished she'd eaten better. She washed another skirt and wondered if she should tell someone. They'd miss her when she died. Her mother might even say, "Maybe I shouldn't have made her clean her room."

Vani's father flicked on the All India Radio news as she came back into the house. Something about cancer rates increasing. Of course. Cancer had claimed Appa's old aunt Komalam the year before. Throat cancer it was, and in the end even talking had been difficult. So no surprise it's caught up with me, thought Vani, feeling pleasantly tragic. She paused by the mirror and looked for signs of doom.

Light fell through the window on her reflection, and Vani paused to wonder at how her body had changed from its comfortable, stocky self. She looked down in surprise. Her skin was translucent—had she known that? A delicate blue vein ran down the front of her chest, disappearing into the gentle swelling of breasts budding beneath her faded green dress. And they hurt, too, felt tight and funny. "Something's happening to me," she decided. "Probably something horrible. But what?"

She found out soon enough. "How many skirts have you washed today?" Amma demanded when she got back from the bazaar, set down the shopping bags bursting with vegetables, and found the clothesline groaning. And when Vani confessed that she had been bleeding all of two days and was about to draw her last breath, Amma sat down on the garage step and laughed and laughed and laughed.

"What?" said Vani. "What's so funny?"

Amma wiped her eyes. "I'm sorry," she said. "You're not dying. You know, I was thinking I ought to explain it all to you one of these days, but it seems your body couldn't wait. Here, let me tell you what to do. . . ." She left the eggplant and green chilies and potatoes sitting out on the gravel. Amma took Vani in, brought down boxes from a shelf high up, and explained how to use the pads.

"In the old days," said Amma, "they used to hold ceremonies to celebrate this. Not anymore, thank goodness. Imagine advertising to the whole world that you've got your period! Here, wear this." And she slipped a silver bracelet onto Vani's wrist. It was a little trellis of leaves and flowers, hammered into a circle, now slightly bent with age. "It's old," said Amma, "from an old friend I lost touch with. I think she'd be happy to know you're wearing it."

"Who was your friend?" asked Vani. "What was her name?"

"Fauzia," said Amma. "She was my best friend."

"Tell me," Vani demanded. "Tell me about her."

They sat and talked until the pigeons cooed an end to the day. Vani's head whirled with images of a country ripped in two, her mother young and scared, and a friendship held together for years by a silver bracelet.

### BALTIMORE, MARYLAND: 1999

It wasn't as if Meena hadn't known. Fourth grade had brought a form for her parents to sign, allowing Meena to attend the session with the school nurse. At the end of it all, she had a packet to take home, and words for the things that were supposed to happen to her body. Mom had glanced over the packet and talked to her solemnly about being prepared and making sure she carried supplies in her backpack in case she started her period when she was in school.

Mom raised it all again as Meena grew taller and her body began to lose some of the angles it had held all childhood long. "Remember that talk we had about periods?" Mom asked. "You're about ready, I think." And Meena caught a certain look on her mother's face, right between a worry and a smile.

"Mom," said Meena. "Why are you looking at me like that?"

"I can't help it," said Mom. "I can't believe how soon you're growing up. Children seem to grow up so much faster now than when I was young."

And Meena replied, dismissing all that, "When you were young, you were in India. Of course it was different."

In the end it happened at night. Meena had gone to bed with an ache in her legs, the kind of ache that her grandmother used to call *kaal-kudatchal,* and treat with sesame oil rubdowns. *Pati,* Meena called her grandmother, the Tamil word for grandma. It conjured her up in Meena's mind with the clarity of a fine portrait—Lakshmi Krishnan, sixty-four years old, white hair, bright eyes. But Pati was in India, not due here for another two weeks, according to the letter that had shown up fatly in the mailbox.

And as it turned out, sesame oil might not have helped.

Thinking about her grandmother, Meena fell asleep. Remembering her from bits and snatches of all those visits to India, Meena tossed about and dreamed of falling into a trough of mango jam. It tasted every bit as awful as it had in India last year. I'm drowning, she thought, I'm drowning in the stuff. She awoke with a start. The sheets were cold, her nightgown bloody. She thought, This is it. This is what it feels like. And then, This is what all the fuss is about?

In two weeks, right on schedule, Pati arrived with enough baggage for an army. Mom and Meena picked her up at the airport.

"Vani, make me a cup of tea," said Pati to Mom. "Those airlines people don't know how to make tea."

As they settled down around the teapot, Mom brought out a small red box. "You still have that?" Pati clapped her hands, more like an excited girl than a dignified grandmother.

Mom said, "I think it should go to Meena, don't you?"

Meena cried, swept up in sudden anticipation, "What? What should go to me?"

Pati murmured, a strum to the music of her granddaughter's exuberance, "After all these years!"

Mom drew from the faded red box a silver bracelet, a frail trellis of leaves and flowers. It was tarnished and dented by years of wearing and forgetting and packing away. To Meena it seemed to carry that mystery that old things have, a sense of having been through time. "For me," she said. "All the way from India." She slipped it on, felt its metallic chill. They sat around the table for a while, watching the wispy steam curl out of the fat teapot, smiling at a battered old silver bracelet on a girl's brown wrist. Mom poured the tea, amber-gold with a bitter fragrance. Indian-style, she dashed milk into each cup, and added sugar to turn it strong and sweet.

"All the way," said Pati, "from 1947. From Fauzia."

"Who's Fauzia?" Meena glanced up to see her mother and grandmother exchange looks. There'll be a story about this, she thought. I can always tell when there's an India story bubbling up.

As if she'd heard the thought, Pati leaned forward, her sharp, dark eyes settling on Meena with a world of promise. She took a sip of tea and a deep breath. "The newspapers had a name," she began, "for what happened to India."

# The Lacts of Fife

Johanna Hurwitz

"All the girls at school are wearing bras," I tell my mom.

"All of them?" she asks. "You're not even twelve yet."

"All of them: Amy, Nicole, Jacki . . ."

"That's three," my mother says. "What about the other nine girls in your class?"

"I don't go peeking at other people's underwear," I reply. "Anyhow, I definitely need a bra, too."

"I don't think they make them that small," she says. Then she sees the expression on my face. "Okay, okay. I'll take you on Saturday."

"Promise?" I ask.

"Promise," she says. I can hardly wait. I know that

if the bra's too big, I can stick Kleenex inside like some of the other girls do.

On Saturday, right after lunch, we start off. The weather is good, and since it's just a few blocks to the ladies' shop where my mom buys her bras and panties, we decide to walk instead of take the bus. As we leave our building, I see Mrs. Saretsky pushing her son Matthew in his stroller.

"How much longer till your birthday?" Mrs. Saretsky asks me.

My parents said I could begin baby-sitting when I turn twelve. Mrs. Saretsky is desperate for a baby-sitter, and I'm just as desperate to earn my own money. Besides, I love little kids, so I know it will be fun.

"Just another month," I say, and give Matthew a grin. He's a really cute kid, and he smiles back at me.

Out on the street, my mother clears her throat. She always does that when she wants to say something but isn't sure how to put it. My mom is a kindergarten teacher, and I think she finds it hard to talk to me ever since I graduated into first grade. And now that I'm in sixth grade, it's gotten worse. She can talk nonstop about her students and their various problems, the situation in Africa or the Middle East, and she can tell you every detail about the politics here in New York City, but she can't say anything to me about personal matters. Really, it's pathetic.

As we walk down the street, my mother says, "You're certainly growing up these days."

"Yep. I'm the second tallest girl in sixth grade. The only one who's taller than me is Ellie Ginsburg, and she wears platform shoes so no one really knows her height, except on the days we have gym when she has to take them off."

"Is that so? I didn't realize that you were so much taller than your classmates. Well, your father is tall, and all the famous fashion models are, too," my mother says.

I pull back my shoulders and try to imagine myself as a future fashion model. It's unlikely, but who knows?

Just then I see two little girls walking toward us holding ice-cream cones. They look around eight years old. It feels like a hundred years since I was that young. I can hardly remember back then. But I still love ice cream, so it gives me an idea.

"Can we stop for ice cream on the way home?" I ask.

Mom has a sweet tooth just like me, so she agrees. The thought of a dish of chocolate ice cream is cheering. I really want a bra, but I'm a bit nervous about trying one on in front of the store assistant and my mom. I'll concentrate on the ice cream. By the time I'm eating it, the embarrassment will be over.

My mother clears her throat again. "Well, as I was saying, you're getting bigger. And do you realize that the inside of your body is growing, too?"

Of course I do. I even sort of guess which direction this conversation is taking. We've had discussions on this subject in health ed at school. And it's something that my girlfriends and I talk about a lot, too. Last month, when Nicole had a sleepover for three girls, we stayed up talking about this kind of stuff for ages. But I don't say any of this to my mother. I just wait to hear what she's going to say next.

"You've gotten your twelve-year-old molars, and you even have the beginnings of wisdom teeth, according to Dr. Levinson," my mother says. I know she feels more comfortable talking about teeth than ovaries. "Funny, though," she goes on, "I never got any wisdom teeth myself. I don't even know why they call them that. They have nothing to do with intelligence. I'm just as smart as the next person, even if I don't have those so-called wisdom teeth."

"You shouldn't feel bad about not having them," I console her.

"You're right. My mother didn't have any wisdom teeth, either. But I think Uncle Jack does."

By now we've reached the corner, so we wait for the traffic light to turn so we can cross Queens Boulevard.

When the light changes, my mother grabs my hand and rushes us across the street.

"Mom! I'm not a baby," I protest, yanking my hand away from her. "You always treat me like one of your kindergarten kids."

She deliberately ignores what I've said to her. She knows I absolutely *hate* having her hold my hand when we cross the street. Instead, when we are safely across the street, my mother says, "Well, let me tell you one thing your uncle will never have."

"What's that?" I ask.

"He won't ever have the chance to have children. So there."

"Maybe he'll get married someday. Then he could have children."

"That's not what I was referring to," my mother says. "He might have children, but he won't *have* them, if you know what I mean. Men aren't blessed with the chance of motherhood."

I giggle. "That would be funny. If men were mothers, who would be the fathers?"

"Anyhow," says my mother. "I think it's time we discussed the Lacts of Fife." Then her face turns bright red and she corrects herself. "Facts of Life," she says loudly, and then looks around to see if anyone on the street has overheard her.

"You mean sex?" I ask.

Now her face turns even redder. "Not so loud," she says to me. "We don't need everyone on the street to hear our conversation."

My mother takes a deep breath. I can see she doesn't know where to begin. "Well, not sex exactly," she says. "But growing up and stuff like that. Well, um. Yes, I guess you could call it sex. Female sex as opposed to male. And it's time we discussed it together."

"Okay. Go ahead," I say.

"Well," she says, clearing her throat, "perhaps you've heard some of the girls at school talking about it already." There's a hopeful tone to her voice.

"A little," I admit.

"So you're aware that one of these days you'll begin menstruating?"

"Sort of," I say. I think I'd need to have lived inside a vacuum not to know anything about all this, but I want to hear what she has to say on the subject.

"Well, it's nothing to be afraid of. It's something

very natural. Every month you'll find yourself bleeding. I'll get you sanitary pads so you won't soil your clothing. It will only last for four or five days each month."

"Four or five days?" I repeat. "How many months does it happen?"

"Until you're somewhere between forty-five and fifty years old, I imagine," says my mother. "Some women even continue until they're older than that."

"Till I'm an old lady?" I gasp. None of the girls at school ever mentioned that this business would go on for practically my whole life.

"Forty-five isn't an old lady!" my mother protests. She's going to be forty-four on her next birthday. And I happen to think that's very old.

"Wait a minute," I say, doing some calculations in my head. "I'm almost twelve. Say I begin this bleeding when I'm thirteen, and continue until I'm fifty. That's thirty-seven years times twelve months is 444 months, and that times five days is 2,220." You can guess that math is my best subject at school.

"You're amazing," my mother says. "You get that from your dad. Maybe you'll become an accountant, too."

I'd rather die than become an accountant. But then I think of those numbers. "Two thousand two hundred and twenty days of bleeding! I'm going to need a blood transfusion to keep me going. I'll die."

"Of course you won't," my mother says. "Look at all the women walking along the street right now. I bet at least a third of them are menstruating at this very moment. They're all going about their business. It's not like being sick. You don't lose that much blood. You'll feel fine."

"Are you?"

"Am I what?"

"Are you bleeding right now?"

"No," she says, but her face is turning red again. I wonder if she's telling the truth.

"What happens to boys?" I ask. "No one ever talks about that."

"What do you mean?" my mother says.

"If girls bleed, what happens to boys? Do they bleed, too?"

"No."

"No? That's not fair at all. Something should happen to them, too," I insist.

"Something does," my mother says, nodding. "Their voices get deeper."

"Big deal. I'd rather have a deeper voice than bleed every month."

"The problem is you don't have a choice," my

mother points out. "Besides, other things happen to boys. They get hair on their faces."

"Yuck." That doesn't appeal to me at all. But it still seems as if boys get away with murder.

"What do *you* call it?" I ask my mother.

"Call what?"

"The bleeding every month. When the girls talk about it at school, they all use different words."

"Like what?" she wants to know.

*"Girlfriend, monthlies, period, curse."* It was Amy who used that last one. She heard her grandmother say it, and I can understand why it's called the *curse.* But the other names sound silly. *Girlfriend?* What kind of a friend is that?

"Those are euphemisms," my mother explains. I can see she is pleased to show off that she knows such an unusual word. "Some people don't like to say *menstruating.*" I smile to myself when she says that. Five minutes ago, she herself could hardly get the word out of her mouth. "You don't have to call it anything at all, if you don't want to," she says now. "You'll see. After a while you'll hardly be aware of it. It'll just be part of your existence, like brushing your teeth or cutting your toenails."

I wiggle my toes inside my shoes. "I don't believe that," I tell her.

"Look at it this way, then," my mother says. "Eventually all these body changes will permit you to conceive a baby. And that's the most wonderful experience a woman could ever have." She smiles at me as she says that. "So," she says, looking relieved that we're finishing this awkward discussion. "Do you have any more questions about any of this?"

"How about telling me where babies come from," I suggest.

My mother looks stunned. So I let her off the hook. Really, it was mean of me to ask her that one, especially since I know it all already.

"Oh, never mind," I tell her. "Here we are at Lilly's Lingerie."

A woman is exiting the shop, pushing a stroller in front of her. Inside is a darling little girl wearing a bright red jacket with a hood. She has curly blond hair and very blue eyes.

"What's her name?" I ask, bending down.

"Sophie," says her mother, beaming at me.

Well, Sophie, I think as I walk into the shop, if I can have a baby like you someday, then I guess it's worth all that mess of being born female. Afterward I think I'll get coffee ice cream. It's more grown-up than my usual chocolate.

# A Family Sandwich

### Jane Kurtz

Today was the second worst day of my whole entire life.

There are some weeks when I actually don't think about the worst one. Well, not whole, entire weeks. But I know for sure there are *parts* of weeks when I'm goofing around like an ordinary person—not a kid whose mom is dead.

She was going to a meeting at my school. I can see her running one hand through her short red hair, making it look like a thistle. She was late. I torture myself by remembering that moment over and over because, as Mom used to say, I've always been perverse.

Her brother from California was visiting. He tossed her the keys to his new Corvette and said, "I know you've been itching to try it out."

My mom caught them like a pro. She looked out the window and laughed. "Your car should zip me there in nothing flat." She kissed the top of my head. "Gotta get going," she said. "When I get back, I'll take you for a spin around the block-o."

She got going all right—right off the road, right off the face of the earth. When Dad told me, my first thought was, That's impossible. Tomorrow is my birthday.

No day in the six months since she died has been great. But today was total yuck, starting with bad hair and going straight to Craig playing with his breakfast again. It was irritating to watch someone who had nothing to do but build Cheerio towers. "Look, Mercedes," he kept saying to me. "Look at *this* one."

Finally, Dad looked. "Eat that stuff," he said. "It will make you big and strong."

"You don't know everything," Craig said.

"I know a few things more than you do." Dad went back to watching the news, which he never did at breakfast when Mom was here.

"That's not everything." Craig grabbed Jesse's truck. Jesse screamed.

I groaned. My parents had only me for seven years

and then thought it was a terrific idea to have two more kids right in a row.

"Hey," Dad said. "Give that back."

"He gave it to me," Craig said.

"Noooo," Jesse wailed.

Craig stuck a Cheerio in his mouth. "He just doesn't remember."

Dad took the truck and put it on the shelf. After a few minutes, Craig lifted his foot onto the table. "Want a toe jam sandwich?"

Dad laughed.

"Don't be gross," I said.

"You okay?" Dad asked. "Busy day?"

I put my dish in the sink, but I didn't rinse it off. Last night, I thought I heard her coming in the door, fumbling with the key the way she did. But it was only Jesse, lying in his bed and thumping his feet against the wall.

When I got to school, I was still in that mood like when I want to be happy but I can't. "Hey, did you do the algebra?" Devoy asked. She was the kind of girl who would never have said one word to me before I started being all sad and having trouble in school.

I rolled my eyes.

"You know one thing for sure," Devoy said. "I'm behind in every subject."

I was, too. Mom would have had me in the counselor's office. "Sit up straight and take your life seriously," I could hear her saying to me. She'd glance at the counselor over the top of her glasses. She wears—wore—the glasses whenever she wanted to make an extra-important point.

I knew how the counselor would end the conversation. "How should I contact you if there are any more problems?"

Then Mom would say what she always told my teachers. "Send a note home with Mercedes. She's trustworthy." She'd wink at me so the counselor couldn't see. "She knows I'll break both her arms if she lets me down."

By English my mood hadn't gone away. I leaned over to Devoy while Jarrett was giving the definition for *docile*. "He's soooo intelligent," I whispered. "Can anyone believe he knows today's date?"

Devoy giggled. She thought it was funny when I was a smart-mouth about guys who made the other girls get goo-goo eyes. I never told her that I was secretly all goo-goo eyes about Jarrett, too. His mom and my mom were best friends, so he and I grew up in each other's sandboxes, and I was pretty sure he kind of liked me, too.

"Party at my house tonight," Devoy whispered.

I felt bad then. Had being sarcastic about someone I like just gotten me invited to a cool person's party?

On my way home, I realized it was my turn with Jesse and Craig. Some evenings, I took care of them while Dad caught up with work. That way, he could take off afternoons. "Would you trade Sunday for tonight?" I asked while we were cleaning up after dinner. "There's this . . . sort of party."

Dad flicked me with his towel. "Go ahead. It would be just fine, you know, if you could start to have fun again."

I knew he was looking at me, but I refused to look back. "You know, Mercedes," he said, "you're lucky that you had—what? Eleven years with your mom? I mean, Craig remembers her as perfect."

"She *was* perfect," I said flatly. I knew she wasn't, but I wasn't in the mood to hear any criticism about her. I thought about the funeral. Mom liked to go to church—she really did. But what could the preacher say? "This was a woman who didn't volunteer to clean up after potluck dinners"? She wasn't a docile woman. As many times as I saw Dad rub her neck, I heard them arguing.

Devoy's house was only eight blocks away, so I walked. The first thing I saw when I got inside was Devoy's mom putting out snacks, and I felt a big hand squeeze my insides like a washcloth. Who would put out snacks at my parties? The next thing I saw was Devoy and Jarrett dancing with each other. Well, why not? It wasn't like he was my boyfriend or something. He smiled and waved at me, but I just pretended I didn't see. Why was I being so perverse? I'd been that way the whole entire day. I wandered off to Devoy's bathroom— and that's when I realized what today was all about.

At first, staring at the blood, I didn't even get it. For one thing, it looked darker than what I think of when I hear the word *blood*. And I didn't instantly connect with Mom reading to me on my bed, joking and laughing, calling the book "that Susie Hamster book," asking me, "Who thought this was a good book for moms and daughters to talk about menstruation?" She could hardly wait. We were going to do a ceremony when that big day came— she and her friends and me in a warm and huggy circle.

I stared into the mirror, watching tears ooze out of my eyes. I was an orphan. A flat-out orphan. This might even be worse than my birthday the day after Mom died.

Okay. What would Mom do? She'd go ask someone for help, of course. I felt clumsy and stupid, but I folded up some toilet paper, stuffed it in my underwear, and went clattering downstairs to look for Devoy.

The good thing was I found her right away. The bad thing was she was in her kitchen. Well, that wasn't the bad thing—the bad thing was Jarrett was in the kitchen, too. No, that wasn't the bad thing. The bad thing was I saw Devoy kissing Jarrett on the mouth. He wasn't my boyfriend or anything, but, still, I could hear my heart pull apart into two pieces with a soft *riiiiiip* like tearing silk.

I ran through the darkish living room, out the front door—open, bang shut—and down the steps. Behind me I heard the door open and bang shut. "Mercedes," Jarrett's voice called. "Hold up."

I didn't. The door opened and banged shut again. "Jarrett." This time it was Devoy's voice. "Hang on. I need to ask you something."

I was a walking storm, waving my arms, furious with everyone, especially my mother, who just *had* to be late and get into that fast car, who had to talk to me about huggy ceremonies and then leave me completely and totally alone. I was halfway home when I heard Jarrett running and panting behind me. He caught up right before we got to my house. "So," I said, not stopping. "What did she want to ask you?"

"She wanted to ask me, 'How did I do?'" There was just enough moon that I could tell, if I looked at him, whether he was smiling or not.

"How *did* she do?" I asked.

"Mercedes—"

"How did she *do*?" I planted my feet and gave him a fierce look.

"I thought it was a good-styled kiss, but how would I know?" He wasn't smiling. "I haven't been kissed since you kissed me in third grade. Except by my mom."

I was mad at his mom . . . and my mom. They belonged here with me in the moonlight. "We'll have a ceremony," Mom had said. "All the wise women of your life around you in the moonlight. We'll howl like she-wolves. We'll dance an ancient woman-power dance."

I remember staring at her, trying to tell if she really meant it. "How will we know the steps?" I'd asked.

"We'll make them up."

Right in the middle of the moonlight, I gave Jarrett the best-styled kiss I could. "There," I said. "Now you have something to compare." I went inside, laughing like a she-wolf.

Dad was on the couch, reading. I stood there twisting my fingers together, trying to figure out what to say, when I heard Craig's footsteps clomping down the hall. "What are you doing now?" Dad hollered.

"I ate a strawberry," Craig called back. "I have to brush my teeth again."

"No, you don't. Go to bed."

Craig poked his head into the living room. "The dentist told me to brush my teeth if I eat something before I go to bed."

"The dentist told me not to let you play games with me."

"That was *your* dentist." Craig disappeared again.

Dad stood up. "If you get up again," he yelled, "I'm going to spank you."

I looked at Dad. He looked at me. Mom and Dad had promised each other, no spanking. It was one of the few things they agreed on. Suddenly Craig shouted, "This is not a game. I need to pee."

Dad stormed out of the room. "That's it."

Craig started to wail. "Mom told me I could go to

the bathroom." He cried harder. "Don't . . . say . . . you're . . . going . . . to . . . spank . . . me."

I was bawling, too, when Dad came back into the living room carrying Craig, whose legs hung down below Dad's knees. Dad dropped onto the couch and pulled me down beside him. "Sorry," he said. "I'm sorry, you guys."

I leaned into him, and his neck smelled warm and dadlike. "She wasn't perfect," I snuffled into his ear. She didn't always pay her library fines. She almost always said exactly what she was thinking. "She was just, you know. A human being."

Jesse stumbled in, rubbing his hair. Mom didn't think having three kids was a terrific idea. Once she told Jarrett's mom that having a big family is like spending your day herding worms.

"Come here, Jesse," Dad said. Craig held out his arms. Jesse climbed onto Craig's lap. "We made a sandwich," Jesse said.

"Yeah." Dad rubbed his head. "You and I are bread. Craig is baloney. What's Mercedes?"

I wasn't going to be some thrown-out piece of lettuce or something. This family was counting on me for woman power now. "Are you ever going to let me have a party here?" I asked him. "A real girl-boy party, I mean?"

"Maybe," he said. "Maybe when you're twenty-one."

I blew my nose, grinning into the Kleenex. Dad didn't know the education he had ahead of him. First he was going to take me to the store for supplies. And if I got too embarrassed, he was the one who was going to buy them. After that he and I were going out in the moonlight. In my mind I was already making up the steps—forward, backward, sideways, dip . . . the steps to a whole, entire, ancient father-and-daughter dance.

# Betrayal
Bobbi Katz

Long before the small circle of my life had expanded to include school and Patty O'Donavan, our family moved into a newly built, two-family brick house. I remember every detail of our first-floor apartment, from the hardware on the front door to the way the light streamed into the back sunroom. I remember the patterns of long-gone wallpapers, bedspreads, floor coverings.

And I particularly remember a March day exactly six weeks before my eleventh birthday. The white wicker clothes hamper in the bathroom was no longer straight against the wall but catty-cornered. Behind it was a big blue box of something called Kotex. I examined the strange white objects in the box. Covered in gauze, they looked like thick little mattresses for a dolls' hospital. Turning one over, I saw the two narrow sides had extensions: thin sleeves that were neatly folded behind the thick part. They opened up, so the mattress was more like a hammock. I knew they were neither, but what could they be?

"Nothing children need," said my sister, Phyllys, who was six years older. She had bras, lipstick, high heels for special occasions, and two collections I was not supposed to touch—fancy perfume bottles and sugar cubes wrapped in papers. The names of hotels and restaurants were printed on them. But even when full of grown-up superiority, Phyllys usually could be depended on for honesty. "Nothing children need." Were those white things shoulder pads?

After trying on a pair with my sweater, I had to admit she was right. Here were fashion items I was simply too young to appreciate. Or *were* they shoulder pads? The contents of the big blue box would diminish and suddenly disappear. A new box appeared. Where were those shoulder pads going?

When asked, Mother tersely explained, "They are for when you are unwell." Obviously, they were not to be taken with water like a pill, but it was equally clear to me that Mom wasn't going to say any more on the subject.

Patty O'Donavan and I had discovered each other in first grade. On the way home from school, we had so much to talk about that even though I should have turned off for my street three blocks before her house, I often walked almost all the way to her house, or she walked almost all the way to mine. By second grade we had taken an oath to be best-friends-for-life. Since we weren't sure whether we were going to be detectives or veterinarians, we prepared for both careers. We copied license plate numbers of suspicious-looking cars and did our best to save baby birds that fell out of their nests. Unfortunately, no matter how careful we were, our patients all died.

Wrapping each stiff bird in a small cotton handkerchief, we buried several right behind the lilac bushes at the side of my house. We dug a little grave with an old serving spoon. Patty said an "Our Father"; I recited a Hebrew blessing, the *brochah* for sabbath candles. However, after Patty had gone to a proper wake and funeral, she was no longer satisfied with our ceremonies. A shoebox coffin was not something we could easily bury. Naturally, when I showed Patty the mysterious pads and told her what my mother had said, she was delighted. After all, what could be more "unwell" than a dead baby robin?

The next time death struck, I pirated a white pad, and Patty placed the deceased on it. We sat on the damp ground with our heads bowed during the "viewing," which was unnoticed by any of the bird's feathered family. Several small ants showed casual interest, but no others. Then, each holding an end of the pad, Patty and I carried the bird to its grave.

Although it was less than a foot away, it was tricky to keep the stiff little bird from falling off its bier. Patty added the words *Dominus nobiscum* after the "Our Father," and I did the usual Hebrew *brochah*.

I was a little nervous about my theft during dinner, although I had a ready defense: The bird was "unwell." But nobody said a word.

The next day at recess, Patty reported that she had discovered her mother had a box marked Kotex behind the towels in the linen closet. It was just like the one at my house! A better detective than I, she had already checked the big dictionary. *Kotex* was not there. She was going to ask her mother about it. Meanwhile, since she couldn't come to my house after school that day, she wanted me to promise to visit the grave of the departed.

A light rain had fallen, and the ground was damp. I sat beside the lilac bushes, trying to feel properly mournful. I thought of the birds we had buried.

Were they all in some robin heaven, chirping and flying?

My throat was a little scratchy the next morning, but I could hardly wait to get to school. Patty, however, was avoiding me. Confused, I pursued her. Yes, her mother had told her all about Kotex, but she had to promise not to discuss it with anyone. "But I am your best-friend-for-life!" I argued. Nothing I said could convince Patty to tell. For the first time since first grade, we did not walk even part of the way home together after school.

By supper time my throat was so sore that all I had was a cup of chicken soup and a dish of red Jell-O. The next morning Mom decided that I should stay home. She had to go to work, but she left me a pitcher of pineapple juice in the refrigerator and four cups of green Jell-O. She reminded me it was the day the insurance man came to collect the monthly premiums. Instead of leaving the money on the table in the hall, she counted on me to give it to him.

At first it was rather lovely to be all alone at home. I sat at my mother's dressing table, opening all the little drawers, brushing my eyebrows with the tiny black mascara brush, and curling my eyelashes. I tried on a little crocheted evening cap jeweled with bronze beads and experimented with a paper fan. At noon I turned on the radio and listened to the soap operas I had gotten used to when my grandparents lived with us: *Helen Trent*, which asked if a woman could find love after the age of thirty-five, and *My Girl, Sunday*: "Can this girl from a little mining town in the West find happiness as the wife of Lord Henry . . . ?" I liked poor old Helen, but I didn't care a fig about Sunday.

My throat felt worse and worse. The cold juice didn't make it feel any better; neither did the Jell-O. It hurt to swallow. And then I remembered!

Taking a pad out of the big blue box, I tried tying it around my neck. Not a good fit. I needed a pin. There were such nice pins in Mother's jewelry box, but I didn't want to borrow something valuable without asking, especially since I had a way of losing things. Then I thought of the big metal hair clips that Mom used before she went someplace special. She wet her hair and combed in some good-smelling, gooey stuff. Next came the clips: one, two, three; big, medium, small. In a couple of hours she took them out, and there were three nice waves, one behind the other, right on the top of her head.

I needed only one clip to hold the pad in place around my neck. The medium fit nicely beneath my chin. I settled down on the living-room couch, waiting to feel better. And waiting.

The doorbell rang. The insurance man, the good-looking youngish one, seemed confused. His mouth was open, but he wasn't saying anything.

"I'm unwell," I said. I drew my hand to my throat as I gave him the money. After he marked our payment card, I asked if he'd like to come inside for some pineapple juice. "No, thanks," he said. "I have to be on my way. Lots of customers. Lots of collections."

After he left I was trying to figure out if the pad would work better with the clip in the back. That's when Phyllys arrived from high school. She didn't even ask how my sore throat was. She took one look at me and started to holler. "What do you think you're doing? You're disgusting. Wait until Mom hears. You take that off now."

But no. I railed against the injustice. I needed that pad. "I'm unwell. My throat hurts."

"I'm calling Mom, Smarty Pants," said Phyllys. And she did. After Phyllys had her say, she gave me the phone. Mom didn't sound angry at all.

She just told me to take the pad off. It wasn't going to help my throat. We would have a talk after supper.

And we did. I wish that it had been a private talk without Miss Big Mouth Phyllys. Mom asked me if I knew what menstruation was. I said I didn't, but Phyllys kept insisting I did. Mom believed me and explained. Stunned, I sat there, trying to take in what she was telling me.

For eleven years I'd had this body I thought I knew. Now I was finding out it was booby-trapped. It was all I could do to keep the giant roar of outrage, betrayal, and embarrassment inside of me. I was furious at Phyllys, furious at Patty O'Donavan, furious at my deceitful body. I went to bed churning and churning with anger, unable to sleep.

Two days later, when I was back at school, I could hardly look at my best-friend-for-life. How could she have kept such an awful secret from me? At the very least, she could have spared me the humiliation of the insurance man.

Yet before long the power of our shared adventures pulled me toward Patty again. We walked home together, but we never buried another bird. On my birthday I was invited to her house after school. Using dishes normally kept behind glass in the china closet, Mrs. O'Donavan served us tea and cakes, as if we were young ladies. However, something had broken between Patty and me.

That summer I went to a new sleep-away camp. In my bunk you hardly knew someone's name before she was asking if you had started to get your period. I didn't write Patty long letters like I had from Camp Echo—just a postcard that anyone could read.

In the fall we both started middle school in different classrooms. At first we walked home from school together, but gradually we discovered that going in different directions suited us. That January, when I had my first period, it never even occurred to me to tell Patty O'Donavan or to ask if she had gotten hers.

As for the insurance man, I saw him many times. I just hoped he didn't see me.

# Hurry Up and Wait
## By Erzsi Deàk

Bobby Vee's song "Come Back When You Grow Up" was still on the radio that year. It was 1972 and I was twelve years old, on the verge of growing up—if only I would start my period and could get my ears pierced. But there wasn't a thing I could do to make my period start, and Mom was sick of hearing about earrings.

Finally, Mom and I made a deal. "Zoë," she said one day after I'd harassed her about piercing my ears for the millionth time, "this is what we'll do. You can get your ears pierced when you turn thirteen or when you get your period, whichever comes first."

"I can?" I asked, all the fight seeping out of me. I hadn't expected her to be so reasonable.

"Sure."

While I was waiting for my real life to begin, I couldn't get that song out of my head, and I couldn't get four-year-old Ned out of my hair. I was endlessly baby-sitting him and my other brother, Will. Will was nine, into HotWheels and burping with his best friend, Fred.

A couple of months after Mom and I made the deal, I was thumbing through a pamphlet about "becoming a woman" and watching Ned color the chain of pirate paper dolls I had cut out for him. Bobby Vee's song oozed out of the radio. I dropped the pamphlet and punched the "off" button.

Ned stopped coloring. "Don't you like that song anymore, Zoë?" he asked.

"I'm kind of tired of it." I didn't want to hear any more about not being grown up. Luckily, my best friend, Jamie, came in the door without knocking. Jamie's the youngest of three girls, and when she's not riding her horse, she loves to baby-sit Ned.

"Hi, Ned," she said, kneeling down. "What are you coloring?"

Ned held up his pirates.

"Great job!" Jamie said.

I rolled my eyes. "Let's go upstairs, Jamie. Ned, you wanna come or stay here?"

"Here," he said, coloring furiously.

In my room Jamie flopped on the floor, flipped through the *Seventeen* magazine lying there. I sat on the edge of my bed, shoving aside the pile of information pamphlets that the school nurse, my doctor-parents, and my aunt had given me. I unfolded a thin-papered instruction sheet from a Tampax box and tried to understand the diagram.

"Did you get yours yet?" I asked, like I did every day.

"My what?" Jamie said with a yawn.

"Jamie! Your period. Did you get it?"

"Nope. I hope it never comes." She stopped turning pages and leaned in closer to the magazine. I knew she was reading the article about the girl jockey.

"I wish mine would come—then I could get my ears pierced." I lay back on my bed and stared up at the ceiling. "I am so tired of people thinking I'm just twelve."

"But you *are* twelve."

"I know, but I want to see movies like *The Last Picture Show*, and Mom says, 'Not until you're grown up.' And I have to be thirteen or get my period before I can pierce my ears. Jamie, my life is on hold!"

"Your birthday's next week," Jamie said without looking up.

"I don't think I can wait that long for earrings." I sighed, throwing my arm across my eyes.

"Yuck," said Jamie. "Pierced ears hurt. Think about all that blood." She shivered. "I'm perfectly happy being twelve and having hole-less ears. And I've seen what happens when you get your period. Both my sisters become monsters."

"I'll be nice to you when I get my period."

Jamie snorted. "Just you wait!"

"I *am* waiting! I've been waiting for twelve years, eleven months, and sixteen days!"

Finally, it happened.

Thirteen years to the minute.

My birthday.

My ear-piercing, lucky-number-thirteen birthday.

As I sat down at the family dinner table for my celebration feast, Will thrust a squishy package at me. "Happy Birthday," he growled.

"Thanks." I squeezed it. "I think."

Will wiggled his ears and said, "You're gonna love it. You can give me one on my birthday."

I opened the package slowly. Out popped a slug-like creature.

"It's a Jelly Pal!" Will shouted, grabbing it. "Isn't it the best? Look, it moves just like a real slug, but it's not as slimy! Ned, catch!"

Ned reached to catch the Jelly Pal, missed, and scrambled to pick it up. Cat hair clung to the toy. "Is it candy?" he asked, and stuck it in his mouth.

"No!" Will wailed. "You don't eat it. You freak people with it! Like this." Will snatched the slug and shook it in my face. I rolled my eyes.

"I want it! It's mine!" Ned lunged for my present, knocking Will off his chair as Dad came into the dining room and Mom set the pot of spaghetti on the table.

"Quit it, you two," Dad said, sitting down and unfolding his napkin. "Give Zoë back her present."

I rolled my eyes for the hundredth time that day. "I am so tired of these immature children."

Dad laughed and handed me a small, silver box. "Go on, open it. It's from your mom and me."

I unwrapped the paper carefully, took the lid off the box. Inside sat the tiniest, most delicate amethyst earrings. "They're beautiful, Dad! Mom!" I got up and hugged them both. "Now I'm ready to pierce my ears."

"I thought you might be," Dad said. "I'll get the catgut after the cake."

"Catgut?" I gulped.

"Cool," Will said, tossing the Jelly Pal between his hands. "Catgut. I can't wait to tell Fred."

"You will not tell Fred!" I snapped, and inhaled my spaghetti, while the others took forever to finish. I tapped my foot. I wanted to get to the ear-piercing part of the evening.

Finally Mom brought out a lemon cake with thirteen candles, and everyone sang the Birthday Song. Dad sipped his coffee.

"Can we pierce my ears now?"

"Sure. I'll get my medical bag from the study."

I headed to the bathroom. Will and Ned were right behind me. "Mom," I whined, "the boys are following me!"

"Will! Ned! Leave your sister alone," Mom yelled from the kitchen.

Dad came around the corner and nearly tripped over our cat, Fang, and the two boys. "That cat belongs in the garage, boys," bellowed Dad. "Zoë, in here."

We ducked into the bathroom. He shut the door and locked it. I could hear Will say, "Catgut! Fang-gut!"

"Not Fang!" Ned howled.

"Get that cat to the garage!" Dad shouted through

the bathroom door. Then he rolled his eyes just the way I do.

"Is this going to hurt?" I asked.

"Probably, but not for long. This is the least painful method. Catgut is just surgical thread." He swabbed my ear with alcohol. Then he lit a match, heated the needle, and threaded it. I quivered like the Jelly Pal. "Hold your breath and think about those new earrings you can wear in a month."

"A month?"

"Yup."

"You mean, thirty whole days?" I asked.

"Uh-huh. Hold still." He held my chin and looked at me before he pinched my right ear lobe, stuck the needle through, and tied the loop of thread with a surgical knot. I gritted my teeth and winced. Menstrual cramps wouldn't have anything on this, I thought, looking in the bathroom mirror and admiring the loop of bloody string hanging from my ear. It resembled a small hoop earring—if you didn't look too closely.

Dad held my chin again and eyed me. "Have to make sure they're balanced—you don't want one earring up here and the other hanging down by your shoulder!" I held my breath and didn't move while he pierced the second ear.

"That's it," Dad said. "Clean them with alcohol twice a day, and make sure to roll the loops back and forth a lot. If you don't, your ears will get infected and fall off." He washed his hands, closed up his medical bag, kissed my forehead, and left the bathroom.

"Is that what you say to all your patients?" I called after him.

"Just the ones getting their ears pierced," he said, smiling back at me.

At school the next day, my friends huddled around me.

"You are so lucky, you got your ears pierced!" said Margaret.

"Does it hurt?" asked Susan, brushing aside her thin blond hair to see better.

"When do you get to wear real earrings?" asked Jamie.

"In a month. My mom and dad gave me these teeny-weeny, wonderful little amethyst earrings— my birthstone," I said. And then I gasped.

Margaret, Susan, and Jamie stared at me. "Are you okay?" they all asked at once.

"She looks pale," said Margaret.

"Maybe she's lost too much blood from her ears."

Susan twisted a strand of hair.

"What's going on, Zoë?" Jamie asked.

"Cramps," I squeaked.

"Cramps!" they cried.

"Do you think . . . ?" Susan started.

"No way! First, you get your ears pierced—and now you get cramps? Totally unfair," said Margaret.

"You can have the cramps. I'm going to check to see if it's you-know-what." I headed to the girls' bathroom with my friends scurrying next to me.

"Do you want to go to the nurse?" asked Susan.

I took a deep breath. "No, it's okay. If it's started, I have what I need." I pushed through the swinging door.

"We'll stand guard," Susan and Margaret said, as if we were going in to smoke like some of the ninth graders did.

Jamie followed me into the cubicle. "What do you have?" she asked.

"You know all those ads about being a modern woman?" I said.

"Uh-huh . . . ," she said.

"Well, this is the answer." I held up a tiny, squished tampon. "This is how you can be a modern woman, even when you have your period."

"A tampon! Won't that hurt? My mom only gave me a mini-pad."

"It's not supposed to hurt. Mom let me choose what I wanted to use. I don't need those pads or belts, right?"

"I guess. I'll give you some privacy. I don't think I want to see this." Jamie backed out of the cubicle.

"Right." I clicked the cubicle door shut and took a deep breath before I checked for the telltale spot. "It's here," I said, ripping open the paper wrapping and slipping out the crumpled cardboard-covered tampon. The instructions said to position yourself so it went in easily. I angled myself with one foot on the wall. Here goes, I thought. Yow! The instructions didn't say anything about pain. I tossed the empty cardboard container, swallowed hard, and concentrated on gathering my stuff.

"There!" I threw open the door and tried to walk normally.

"You're limping," Jamie said.

"I don't know if I got this thing in right," I answered, and took another deep breath.

"Can you walk?"

"Sure. I mean, it was only a tiny little spot and the cramps are gone now."

"Yeah," Jamie said. "You can walk like a crab."

"Ouch. Don't make me laugh." I held my middle and winced.

Margaret and Susan ran into the bathroom.

"Hurry up! You're going to be late for second period!"

"How can she be late?" Jamie shot back. "She just got her first period!"

After school Mom picked me up in our old VW bus with the creaky doors. I got in the front seat like I was older than my grandmother.

"What's wrong with you?" my mother asked.

"I got my period," I said. "And I think those tampons are too big!"

Mom hugged me. "Zoë! Now you're a real woman!"

I groaned. "Mom, could you stop squeezing me? This is very uncomfortable." My cheek was pressed against her shoulder, and her love pats reverberated through my body like small explosions.

She pulled back with a big grin on her face. "This is so wonderful. Something only you and I can share—"

"And all the rest of the women in the world."

Mom started the car. The road wasn't exactly smooth. I sat on my hands to ease the agony.

"We'll have a second party tonight. A coming-of-age party," said Mom as we walked into the house.

"Do we have to?" I said, thinking of my brothers.

"Of course! This is a big deal. It only happens once in your life. What kind of cake do you want—strawberry?"

"Anything but red!" I trudged upstairs.

"Don't forget to disinfect your ears," Mom called after me.

"I won't," I said, and collapsed on my bed.

When I woke up, Mom was calling everyone to the table. I went down the stairs very slowly, hanging on to the banister, and sat down at the table, carefully, next to Dad.

Dad carved the roasted chicken. Ned and Will argued about which character was the good guy in the comic book lying open on the table. I tried to find a better sitting position and nearly fell off my chair when Mom opened the dining room doors with a flourish and said, "I have an announcement to make!"

I swallowed hard. Dad looked up from the chicken.

"Is it another party?" Ned asked.

"In a way," Mom said. She smiled down at me and then at the others around the table. I looked at her in horror. Clearing her throat, she sounded like she was trumpeting the arrival of the queen. "Zoë's a woman today."

Was I breathing? I didn't want to be. I wanted to die right then and there. Evaporate.

"So what?" Ned asked.

"So, it means she can have babies," Will said. "This, I gotta tell Fred! Can we eat now?"

Dad smiled at me. "That's very nice," he said. "Ned, get your fingers out of the potatoes. Will, you won't tell Fred anything. This is your sister's life. If she wants to tell Fred, she can, but not you."

"Oh, all right!" he said, and threw the comic book on the floor.

"Ned, sit up," Dad continued. "Who wants dark meat?"

"I do! I do!" the barbarians yelled, and pounded the table.

"Light meat for me, dear," Mom said.

I couldn't believe that all anyone could think about was dark or light meat. "Dad, getting a period is a big deal," I whispered.

"Uh-huh. Light meat?" He held up a forkful of chicken.

"Yes, please." I tried to get comfortable again. "You're a doctor, so it isn't anything big for you. But I'm your daughter. This is supposed to be important."

Dad smiled. "It is important, Zoë. But, I didn't, uh,

want to embarrass you in front of you-know-who." He rolled his eyes around the table to Ned and Will. They stuck out their tongues and went back to eating.

I shifted my weight and fiddled with one of my ears, wincing. "I don't know if this growing up business is worth it," I mumbled.

"Of course it is," Mom said, spooning broccoli onto Will's plate. "When you're ready, you can have a family, just like this one."

I looked around the table. Dad grinned and clicked the carving knife and fork together like a flamenco dancer saying, "*Olé!*" Mom gazed at me with a glaze-eyed you-are-the-most-wonderful-thing-that-ever-happened-to-me look. Will wiggled his ears and chomped on a drumstick. Ned shoveled mashed potatoes into his mouth and said, "Just like us!"

"Can't wait," I said.

"That's what being a woman is all about," said Mom.

"Hey," Will said, nudging Ned. "Zoë's a woman! Zoë's a woman!"

Ned chanted with Will, "Zoë's a woman! Zoë's a woman!"

"Boys, leave Zoë alone!" Mom commanded.

"May I be excused?" I asked. I wanted to disappear. I wanted to remove the tiniest tampon in the world.

"Of course, honey!" Mom said, and gave me a hug.

Back in my room, I threw the pamphlets in the trash. I was a woman now. "Zoë's a woman. Zoë's a woman." I laughed and twisted the strings in my ears, dancing around my room singing Bobby Vee's song "Come Back When You Grow Up."

Now that I had pierced ears and my period, my real life was sure to happen any minute. But for the moment, I wanted the clock to slow down just a bit. This growing up stuff was going a little faster than I'd bargained for. I wanted to enjoy being thirteen. Hang out with Jamie. Go to dances. Even baby-sit Ned once in a while.

I could wait for the rest—at least until I could wear my real earrings.

# About the Contributors

## CARMEN T. BERNIER-GRAND

*In the 1950s in Puerto Rico some boys believed that a girl couldn't be a* señorita *unless a raw grain of rice got stuck between her breasts. Most mothers didn't feel comfortable talking about menstruation. But they did ask their daughters not to wash their hair while they had their periods because more blood could flow out. As a child, I listened to and sometimes believed these and many other myths about menstruation.*

*Like Carlotita in my story, I had my first period when I was nine and a half. When my mother saw me, she burst into tears, because she thought I was way too young to be menstruating. Luckily, I had a sister who had had many periods and could calmly and frankly explain Doña Rosa to me. Carlotita didn't have such luck.*

Carmen T. Bernier-Grand's main inspiration comes from her years growing up in Puerto Rico. She is the

author of four books for children and young adults—
*Shake It, Morena!*; *In the Shade of the Níspero Tree*; *Poet and Politician of Puerto Rico: Don Luís Muñoz Marín;* and *Juan Bobo: Four Folktales from Puerto Rico*. She now lives in Portland, Oregon, with her husband and bilingual dog. Her son and daughter are in college.

## ERZSI DEÀK

*Music is powerful medicine. It works on memory. Zoë's story is very much like my own. Any resemblance to anyone I know is probably true. The Bobby Vee song "Come Back When You Grow Up" (Liberty Label, 1967) has stayed with me through many periods—embarrassing, grumpy, down-in-the-dumps, happy-to-be-alive. When I heard the song recently, my brothers' chant came rushing back. So, I twisted my earrings and danced around the room. I mean, if you're in the memory, you might as well live it, right?*

Erzsi Deàk is an American writer who shares her Hungarian name with a celebrated werewolf. A journalist for more than twenty years, she now writes in Paris, France, where she lives with her Franco-American husband and their three daughters—who finally don't wince at her accent in French. Her story "Envelope Thief" is featured in the book *They Only Laughed Later*. She is on the board of directors of the Society of Children's Book Writers and Illustrators and is currently working on a middle-grade novel starring Romy Simeon.

## JOHANNA HURWITZ

*I've been waiting for years for my mother to tell me the facts of life. It seems unlikely that she ever will, since she's postponed it this long and now is in her late eighties. Meanwhile, I've become a mother myself, and a grandmother as well. I guess I figured things out on my own.*

Johanna Hurwitz is the author of more than fifty novels for young readers, including *Faraway Summer*, *Dear Emma*, and *The Rabbi's Girls*. She and her husband live in Great Neck, New York, and Wilmington, Vermont. They have a daughter and a son who have a son and a daughter.

## FLORENCE JOHNSON JACOB

Florence Johnson Jacob, who was born in 1889, grew up on farms in Arizona and Utah with her sisters, Adeline and Grace, and their three younger brothers. As her granddaughter, I got a big kick out of her twinkling eyes as she told me the story of her first period. Menstruation was a big secret in 1902; Florence's mother and older sister never told her a thing about it. They figured she'd find out soon enough (and she did).

In 1910 Florence married a good-looking hydraulics engineer who traveled all over the West, checking on streams and rivers. When he died suddenly of appendicitis in 1923, Florence became a teacher to support her four children. She never had a book published, but she told stories to her students, children, and grandchildren. During her long life, she wrote hundreds of letters to her family, most of which she saved for later generations to read.

—Kristin Embry Litchman

## BOBBI KATZ

*Once I saw the connection between the letters on my chunky little alphabet blocks and the labels on cans of food in the kitchen cupboard, I learned to read. It was my good fortune to grow up when the radio brought jazz right into our family living room. I've been in love with rhythm and rhyme ever since. As a mom, I discovered illustrated books for children, and began writing for young people—picture books, young novels, and especially poetry.*

*When I heard an American in Paris was collecting "period pieces," faces and feelings from long ago pell-melled into my mind as if they were just happening. My throat was an aching tangle. I wanted to tell my menstruation story.*

Bobbi Katz has worked as a fashion editor, a social worker, and a political activist. Her home base is now in New York City, but she spends lots of time in the mid–Hudson Valley, where she grew up and where she teaches a college course in literature, when her publishing commitments allow. She has published more than sixty books. Her most recent collections of poetry include *We the People* and *A Rumpus of Rhymes: A Book of Noisy Poems. Once Around the Sun* and a collection of first-person poems about explorers will be published soon.

## UMA KRISHNASWAMI

*This story began with an old loss—not mine, but my mother's. I overheard the real-life version as I cultivated the fine childhood habit of eavesdropping on adult conversation. My mother really did have a Muslim friend who left India in 1947, and with whom she then lost contact. It is still an unfinished chapter in her life. In a strange way, national crises and wars make young people grow up suddenly, so that their coming-of-age also becomes a moment in history. In life, as in this story, it sometimes takes generations to transform that history into something to be lived with rather than suppressed or forgotten. But it can happen.*

Uma Krishnaswami was born in New Delhi, India. Her books include *Hello Flower* and *Yoga Class;* story collections *Shower of Gold, The Broken Tusk,* and *Stories of the Flood;* new picture books *Monsoon* and *Chachaji's Cup;* and a story in the anthology *Soul Searching.* She lives and writes in Aztec, New Mexico, where she also leads writing workshops for young people at a UNESCO–designated World Heritage Site, Aztec Ruins National Monument. She is married and has one son.

## JANE KURTZ

*My mom is alive and strong in her seventies—learning Spanish, traveling (to Eastern Europe, Russia, Cuba, India, China, Kenya, and Ethiopia within the last few years), reading interesting books. But I often felt like a motherless child while I was experiencing the emotions and physical changes of the preteen and teenage years. That's because when I was ten years old, I went to boarding school in Addis Ababa while my mother was "back home," far away in the remote southeast corner of Ethiopia. Most years, I saw my parents only at Christmas and for a few months in the summer. I still vividly remember sitting in a big room with my roommates and friends, listening to the dorm mother explain about menstruation . . . and feeling quite utterly alone.*

Jane Kurtz is a children's author who grew up in Ethiopia and now lives in Kansas. She has written acclaimed picture books and middle-grade novels that capture bits of her own childhood experiences growing up among several different cultures. Her picture book about surviving North Dakota's Red River Flood of 1997, *River Friendly, River Wild,* won a Golden Kite Award for most distinguished picture book text from the Society of Children's Book Writers and Illustrators.

## KRISTIN EMBRY LITCHMAN

*I grew up in Los Alamos, New Mexico, with a bomb-testing father, a mother who wrote children's books, five younger siblings, and a friendly nearby library. "I Don't Wanna Hear It" is a true story; I was horrified when I first heard about the monthly bleeding that would be my fate, because I thought it would interfere with my happy life running around in the canyons that cut through our town. I thought my friends made up the story to scare me, but when my mother and the school nurse came up with the same story, I had to believe it.*

Kristin Embry Litchman and her husband, Bill, have

lived for many years in Albuquerque, New Mexico. They teach old-time square and folk dances at work-shops and dance camps around the country and in Europe, and enjoy the company of their two daughters and sons-in-law and their six grandchildren. Her books for young people include *Secrets!, All Is Well,* and *The Wrong Side of the Pattern.* She served for several years as her state's regional advisor for the Society of Children's Book Writers and Illustrators.

## LINDA SUE PARK

*"White Pants" is based on a true story; the names have been changed to protect the mortified. It provides unquestionable evidence of reincarnation: A person can go on to lead a reasonably happy life even after dying of embarrassment.*

Linda Sue Park, awarded the 2002 John Newbery Medal for *A Single Shard*, writes fiction and poetry for both adults and young people. Her other novels include *When My Name Was Keoko, The Kite Fighters,* and *Seesaw Girl.* She lives in western New York with her husband and two children, all of whom object to her description of her PMS as "moderate."

## DIAN CURTIS REGAN

*Three days after moving to Wichita, Kansas, I went out for a run on unfamiliar streets and noticed a sign: DEAF CHILD AREA. As I looked at it, this entire story came to me. However, the sign was not on Chocolate; it was on Cranberry. Poetic license. . . .*

*When I was a child, a bad case of mumps damaged my hearing and left me partially deaf in one ear. Also, like Annie, when it was my "first time," I felt the need to keep it a secret, as if I were not normal. I mention these things because readers always ask if stories are true, and this explains my answer: "Everything is true and nothing is true." Annie is fictitious, but her story intertwines with mine.*

Dian Curtis Regan is the author of many books for young readers, including *Princess Nevermore, The Monster of the Month Club* quartet, and *The Friendship of Milly and Tug.* She has lived in Colorado, Texas, Oklahoma, and Venezuela, and currently resides in Kansas with her collection of one hundred foster walruses (all unnamed). Visit her online at www.diancurtisregan.com

## CYNTHIA LEITICH SMITH

*What I remembered most was the stream water, how cold it was, how clean. The way it tasted through my teeth and on my tongue. For two weeks each summer, I went horseback riding in the mountains surrounding Estes Park. Back then, I could slide my hands into the icy water and scoop it to my lips. But that's not all I remembered. Crisp air. Sudden showers. Mountains, still snow-dusted in July. Cowboys, just enough older to think of me as a kid. But not much older than that.*

Growing up, Cynthia Leitich Smith wanted to be a magician, a vampire, and a disco star. Then she studied to become a newspaper reporter, a public relations professional, and an attorney. She became an author instead. Cynthia's books include *Jingle Dancer, Rain Is Not My*

*Indian Name*, and *Indian Shoes*. She is an enrolled member of the Muscogee (Creek) Indian Nation, and she lives with her husband and two gray tabby cats in sunny Austin, Texas.

Visit her online at www.cynthialeitichsmith.com

## APRIL HALPRIN WAYLAND

*When I was a young teen, my girlfriend Diane and I would fly home after school, drop our books, and rush outside to play for hours with small porcelain elves and plastic animals strategically placed in a corner of my backyard. Some girls ran home to put on makeup and talk about boys. We ran home to play with Bambi and Elfira. I matured later than my peers. I did wonder—and worry—about when my period would come. I asked my friends what it was like to actually get it. And I waited. And waited. And waited. By the time my period came, I was ready. I was probably the last girl on the planet to get a period.*

April Halprin Wayland has been a teacher, a corporate manager, a fiddle player, and a walnut farmer, but she has always been a writer. An award-winning poet, she is the author of several books for younger readers, among them *It's Not My Turn to Look for Grandma!* and *To Rabbittown*. "Period." is from *Girl Coming in for a Landing*, her novel in poems for teens. She teaches in the United States, in Europe, and at UCLA Extension. She and her family live with an odd assortment of animals in Southern California.

# RITA WILLIAMS-GARCIA

*I remember looking forward to getting my period because when my older sister got hers, my mother bought her a suit, new underwear, and a box of sanitary napkins with a rose on the box. Mom kept asking if she was all right and fixed her a lot of tea. Two years later, when I reported my happy news, my mother said, "Oh, Lord, Rita's sick." Then she started to tear up some sheets.*

Rita Williams-Garcia is the author of several acclaimed novels for young adult readers, including *Every Time a Rainbow Dies* and *Like Sisters on the Homefront*, a Coretta Scott King Honor Book. Rita was born in Queens, New York, but grew up in Seaside, California, during the sixties. She received her B.A. degree in liberal arts from Hofstra University and her M.A. in creative writing from Queens College. She works full time for a marketing services company and lives in Jamaica, New York. Rita is the mother of two daughters.